"I'm Sure You And Your Fiancé Will Work It Out.

Especially now that he's about to become a proud papa."

"Oh, I'm pretty sure Paul and I won't be working out anything."

Reid's brows knit at that, but he kept his lips tightly shut. The sooner he distanced himself, the better.

"If running away from the wedding wasn't enough to put an end to things, finding out about this baby sure as heck will be."

He gave a snort of derision. He hadn't meant to, it just sort of came out. "And why is that? I'd think good ole Paul would be even more eager to hustle you down the aisle now that you're pregnant with his kid. Wouldn't an illegitimate heir tarnish his sterling reputation?"

Juliet inhaled deeply, her chest rising as her lungs filled.

"That's just it," she said on a whisper of air. "It's not *his* baby. It's yours."

* * *

Project: Runaway Bride
is part of the Project: Passion series:
For these designing women, love is the latest look.

* * *

If you're on Twitter,
tell us what you think of Harlequin Desire!
#harlequindesire

Dear Reader,

I have always wanted to write a story in which a bride ran away from her wedding because she was pregnant; it just seemed like such a nice twist on the usual reaction of racing *to* the altar when the stick turns blue. And in *Project: Runaway Bride,* I got my chance.

I also got the chance to revisit characters I fell in love with in my first Project: Passion story, *Project: Runaway Heiress.* Lily, Juliet and Zoe easily top the list as three of my favorite heroines, and in *Project: Runaway Bride,* you'll get to know the eldest Zaccaro sister, Juliet, better. She's the sensible one, the responsible one, the one who always does what's expected of her...until she realizes she's walking down the aisle to the wrong man.

I hope you enjoy reading Juliet and Reid's story as much as I did writing it!

XOXO,

Heidi

PROJECT: RUNAWAY BRIDE

HEIDI BETTS

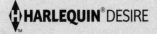

HARLEQUIN®DESIRE

Recycling programs
for this product may
not exist in your area.

ISBN-13: 978-0-373-73293-7

PROJECT: RUNAWAY BRIDE

Printed in U.S.A.

www.Harlequin.com

HEIDI BETTS

An avid romance reader since junior high, *USA TODAY* bestselling author Heidi Betts knew early on that she wanted to write these wonderful stories of love and adventure. It wasn't until her freshman year of college, however, when she spent the entire night before finals reading a romance novel instead of studying, that she decided to take the road less traveled and follow her dream.

Soon after Heidi joined Romance Writers of America, her writing began to garner attention, including placing in the esteemed Golden Heart competition three years in a row. The recipient of numerous awards and stellar reviews, Heidi's books combine believable characters with compelling plotlines, and are consistently described as "delightful," "sizzling" and "wonderfully witty."

For news, fun and information about upcoming books, be sure to visit Heidi online at www.heidibetts.com.

In memory of my grandmother,
Genevieve Gehrlein Stock. She absolutely hated
what I do, and this story probably would have upset
her more than most. But I like to believe that
deep down, she was still proud of me.
So like it or not, Gram, this one's for you!

One

Juliet Zaccaro stared down at the little plastic wand she was clutching between shaky, white-knuckled fingers.

It was one of those kits that promised 100 percent accuracy. No doubts. No second-guessing. And that was definitely a giant blue plus sign, glaring back at her like a flashing Broadway marquee.

She was pregnant.

Her stomach tightened; her lungs following suit. Knees growing weak, she took a single stumbling step sideways and sank onto the closed toilet lid in a cloud of gauzy white crepe and tulle.

A laugh verging on hysterical tickled its way up her throat, but she tamped it down. Pressed her lips together to keep it from spilling out, because she knew if she didn't, she might never stop.

It was her wedding day. Here she was in the cramped

bathroom off the small-but-serviceable room at the rear of the church where she'd been getting ready, and she was very unexpectedly, very this-is-not-good-news pregnant.

She should have taken the test days ago rather than waiting until her hair and makeup were done and she was trussed up in her one-of-a-kind fairy-princess gown designed and hand sewn by her sister Lily. Hadn't she suspected for more than a week now that the dizziness, the headaches, the upset stomachs were more than simply prewedding jitters? But she'd been so afraid she was right, so afraid she might actually be pregnant that she couldn't bear to find out for sure.

And then she'd looked at herself in the mirror, seen herself as a bride about to walk down the aisle and realized she wasn't blushing, she was flushed. She wasn't glowing with happiness; she was radiating dread. And that was just at the prospect of saying "I do."

When she stopped to consider the fact that she might indeed be pregnant, all of her doubts, all of her fears, all of her second thoughts just grew louder and louder until they were a nearly deafening cacophony inside her head. That was when she knew she couldn't wait any longer to take the test and find out for sure.

Now she knew…but she had no idea what to do about it. She couldn't very well walk down the aisle and start a new life with a man who most likely wasn't—most likely? Who was she kidding?—*definitely* wasn't the father of her child.

Dear God, her *child*. A baby. She was really and truly pregnant. Which meant it wasn't just about her anymore. She wasn't going to be the only one affected by whatever decisions she made from this moment forward. She had to start thinking like a mother, putting her child's safety and happiness ahead of her own.

A tap on the bathroom door startled her out of her deeply spiraling dark thoughts. She lifted her head as her sister's muffled voice came from the other side.

"Juliet. We're ready for you, sweetie," Lily said. "It's time to become Mrs. Paul Harris."

Her words were happy, encouraging, meant to uplift. Instead, they made Juliet's stomach drop.

She didn't know if she *could* become Mrs. Paul Harris. Or even if she should.

Taking a deep, shuddering breath, she called out, "I'll be right there. Just one more minute."

"All right. We'll be waiting in the vestibule."

Juliet waited until her sister's faint footsteps trailed off and the outer door closed. Then she pushed herself to her feet with the help of the porcelain vanity and glanced at her reflection in the mirror above the sink.

Not bad, as long as everyone waiting in the pews out front was expecting a Corpse Bride. Every ounce of color had leeched out of her skin, making the eye shadow, rouge and lipstick her sister Zoe had so carefully applied look like that of a practiced geisha.

Brushing a finger beneath each of her eyes, she wiped away any lingering trace of unshed tears and made sure her eyeliner and mascara were still intact. Then she fluffed out the diaphanous folds of her gown and dropped the plastic test stick into the small wicker wastebasket beside the sink. A second later, she leaned down and shook the basket so the wand fell to the very bottom. She certainly didn't want someone accidentally finding a positive pregnancy test in the bridal staging area and taking the time to put two and two together.

As ready as she was ever going to be, she left the bathroom and crossed the main room, slowly turning the knob and opening the outer door only a crack. The hallway was empty, thank goodness. Another moment's reprieve.

Opening the door the rest of the way, she stepped out. The muted whispers of her sisters and father reached her from where they were waiting only a few yards away.

Turn left and she would be at the start of the aisle, stepping her way into a new life to the strains of "The Wedding March."

Turn right toward one of the church's side doors and she could escape. It would be a new life of sorts, too, but one about which she was much less certain.

Her chest rose and fell with her increasingly shallow breaths. Her heart began to race like a greyhound after a rabbit.

Left or right? Go through with the wedding and her promise to Paul, or throw it all away and dive headfirst into the great unknown?

Time seemed to slow as her ears filled with the hollow, echoing sound of ocean waves. And then she did the only thing she could do. She turned right…

…and ran.

Two

Three months earlier...

His intercom buzzed.

"Mr. McCormack, Juliet Zaccaro is here to see you."

Reid's fingers paused over the keyboard in mid-stroke. He tried to tell himself that the clenching of his gut and the flush of heat that washed over him were nothing more than surprise. Her visit was unscheduled and completely unexpected after all.

Pressing the return button on his multiline phone, he cleared his throat and said, "Thank you, Paula. Send her in."

Saving the document he'd been working on, he shuffled some papers off to the side of his desk, then turned his attention to the door as soon as the knob turned and it began to open.

As it had from the first time he'd met her, the sight of Juliet Zaccaro slammed him dead center. Like a race car hitting the wall at a hundred and sixty miles per hour.

She was classically, amazingly beautiful. Flawless skin covered every inch of her strong but smooth features. Her eyes were robin's-egg blue, surrounded by long, dark lashes. And her honey-blond hair, which he suspected would fall well past her shoulders, was always swept up in a neat twist or bun or other type of regal style.

It was enough to make him want to take it down, run his fingers through the silken strands and then strip her of her perfectly tailored, dignified pantsuit, or blouse and skirt, or whatever other prim and proper outfit she might be wearing.

They'd never been anything but professional and courteous with each other, but since the moment they'd met, his fantasies had been ripe with images of having her naked and writhing beneath him. He wanted to crack through her ladylike demeanor to find the not-so-ladylike woman underneath. The one who would wrap her arms and legs around him like a vise, begging him to take her harder, faster, deeper. The one who would rake her nails down his back and scream his name when he sent her hurtling over the edge into bliss.

A wave of heat assailed him, and he prayed she wouldn't notice his intense reaction to her presence as he rose to meet her. Staying behind his desk—flimsy protection though it was—he waited for her to cross the room before offering his hand. Not the first time they'd shaken hands. Not the first time he'd touched her.

Keep it professional, McCormack.

But as his large fingers engulfed her much smaller

ones, as rough, tanned skin surrounded pale and delicate, he wanted to tug her closer, hold on a bit longer, stroke his thumb back and forth along the dip of her palm.

She'd been to his office a handful of times now, and he remembered what she'd been wearing each and every one of them. Today, it was a simple lavender dress with a scoop neckline and narrow belt of the same fabric at her waist. Matching lavender pumps and a few simple pieces of gold jewelry completed the look.

There was an air of Audrey Hepburn or Jackie O to her, something that normally held no appeal to him. Didn't he usually go for flashier women? The kind who knew the score, who were well aware of their sexuality and used it to their advantage. The kind who didn't mind a hot, steamy, short-lived affair.

Juliet Zaccaro, as far as he could tell, did not fall into that category.

Why, then, did he seem so preoccupied with her? He'd agreed to help her the first time she'd walked into his office, despite the fact that it was in direct opposition and a clear conflict of interest to another case he'd already been working on for her sister Lily. And from that point on, he hadn't been able to get her out of his head.

He'd called her with updates when he didn't really have any new information to impart *and* was supposed to be avoiding contact because of her sister's circumstances and the work he was actually focusing on for Lily. He'd met with her in his office—sometimes at her request, other times at his—when there was no real need.

Now here she was again, showing up without warning, for no official reason that he was aware of. Juliet's request that he find her missing sister was moot now that Lily had returned from Los Angeles and come clean with her family about the reason she'd disappeared for several weeks to begin with. He was still working on Lily's case—accusations that an employee from a rival clothing company had stolen her designs—but even though Juliet was part owner in Zaccaro Fashions, the investigation didn't really require direct contact with her.

But that didn't stop him from being oddly glad to see her again. His heart was pumping as though he'd just hopped off the treadmill after an hour-long workout, but he felt the way he used to as a kid when he got exactly the toy he wanted from the bottom of his cereal box, even though there were six different possibilities.

Clearing his throat, he gestured for Juliet to take a seat, then returned to his own. "Ms. Zaccaro. It's nice to see you again, though I wasn't aware we still had any outstanding business."

Although he thought of her as Juliet in his head, he was always careful to address her as Ms. Zaccaro, keeping things as professional as possible between them, as well as giving *himself* the necessary reminder that she was—or had been, anyway—a client *and* that she was engaged to another man.

She smiled shakily and gave a small sniff. Which was when he noticed the trace of red rimming her eyes and the slight pallor of her skin beneath a light layer of makeup.

His own eyes narrowed. Was she in trouble? Was something going on again that she needed his help with?

Part of him wanted to groan—the last thing he needed

was a legitimate reason to spend more time with her—while another part was almost hoping for the worst.

Licking her glossed lips, she said, "I just wanted to drop by and give you a check for the work you did on my case."

He had the decency to flush at that. He hadn't done any work for her. If anything, he'd fed her bad information and given her the runaround for almost a month. Only because he'd been trying to protect the confidentiality of the case he'd already been working on for her sister, but still. He didn't deserve payment for that.

"You don't owe me anything," he told her roughly. In fact, he owed her the retainer she'd left with him back, and made a mental note to see that it was returned.

"Of course I do." Her words were resolute, but her tone was still shaky. "I hired you to do a job and you did it. To the best of your ability, at any rate," she added with a gentle half smile.

"I lied to you and wasted your time," he said—more sharply than he'd intended out of disgust with himself.

"Only because you were already working for Lily, trying to help her save our company. If it hadn't been for you 'pretending' to look for her, I probably would have taken off and tried to find her myself. And we both know I had no idea which direction she'd even gone, so I would have been running in circles, likely getting into more trouble than I imagined she was in. What you did was noble, and pretty much your only option, given the circumstances."

He made an impolite, noncommittal noise, his mouth turning down at the sides. That wasn't his opinion of the situation at all, and having her describe it in such

a positive, almost heroic light only made him feel like
that much more of a heel.

Ignoring him, Juliet went on. "And you're still help-
ing us, which I think shows you how much confidence
we have in your ability. But those abilities don't come
cheap, and I knew that when I approached you."

Unsnapping the small clutch purse on her lap, she
pulled out a check and leaned forward to slide it across
the desk toward him.

Because he suspected no amount of argument would
sway her, and tearing it up in front of her would be a
ruder gesture than even he was comfortable express-
ing in mixed company, he reached for the check with
no intention of ever cashing the damn thing.

That was when he noticed the bruises. Just a few
small, light discolorations dotting the inside of her fore-
arm.

Anyone else would probably have dismissed them
entirely. People bumped into things all the time, ended
up with bruises of an unknown origin.

But he'd seen too much in his thirty-nine years, was
unfortunately all too familiar with the signs of someone
putting his hands on another person. Domestic abuse,
a down-and-dirty street fight, or simply self-defense
practice, there was a difference between *I bumped into
the armoire* and *somebody grabbed me by the arm with
enough force to leave five perfectly formed fingertip-
shaped marks on my skin.*

His jaw clenched with fury at the thought of anyone—*anyone*—grabbing her in anger. He also hated the
thought of anyone other than himself grabbing her in
passion, but that was not how she'd gotten those bruises.
Not there. Not in that pattern.

His first instinct was to reach out and grab her arm for a closer look. Which was about the worst idea ever. The last thing a person who was already sporting bruises from an aggressor needed was to have some other jerk manhandle her soon after.

So he settled for biting down on his rear molars so tightly they threatened to grind into dust and taking the check she was still holding out to him. Slowly, carefully, while contemplating his next best move.

"Thank you," he murmured, setting the check aside before bringing his hands back to clasp them in front of him. If he kept them together and didn't let go, there was less of a chance he'd end up reaching for her after all.

"Let me ask you something, Ms. Zaccaro," he said, amazed at how calm and composed he sounded when he felt anything but.

"Of course. And call me Juliet, please."

He didn't, but went ahead with what he wanted to know most. "Who put his hands on you?"

He was good at reading faces, body language, all those nearly imperceptible ticks and fidgets that people didn't realize they were making, but that were remarkably telling. Juliet's reaction flashed like a neon sign.

She froze, her eyes widening a fraction as she held her breath. An action he identified by the lack of rise and fall to her chest.

After a minute, the silence so thick he'd have needed a machete to cut through it, she licked her lips and offered a nervous laugh.

"I don't know what you're talking about."

His gaze didn't waver. "Sure you do. Those are fingerprints." He pointed to her arms, which were now pulled tight to her body. "Somebody grabbed you with enough force to leave bruises. Pretty big ones, which makes me think it was most likely a man. Your fiancé, perhaps?"

Just saying the word made his stomach knot. The urge to throttle the bastard wasn't far behind.

"So unless you're taking Krav Maga classes at the gym or got into a nasty spat with one of your sisters over the last bolt of vermillion charmeuse in your stockroom, I'd be willing to bet somebody's pushing you around."

Juliet's eyes filled with tears, and the need to punish whoever had done this to her turned into full-blown bloodlust. His fists clenched, knuckles going white. It took every ounce of restraint he possessed to remain perfectly still. To not stand up, round the desk and pull her into his arms. To not march down to the artillery room and suit up with as much weaponry as he could carry.

He swallowed hard. Took a deep breath and held it to the count of ten, then twenty, before letting it out again.

"Tell me what's going on, Juliet," he said, keeping his voice low, level, and reassuring. "Please."

It was the *please* that did it, he could tell. Despite the moisture gathering at her lashes, she'd been holding on, holding back, determined not to admit anything aloud, especially not to a near stranger.

But on a ragged inhalation of breath, the dam broke. Twin trails of tears rolled down her cheeks and her bottom lip trembled as she started to brokenly confide in him.

"It was Paul," she admitted. "I don't know why he's acting like this. He's always been so kind and considerate. But the closer it gets to the wedding, the more…"

Volatile?

"…impatient he seems to be. The tiniest thing can set him off. And whenever we discuss the future—our careers or where we'll live—he gets so angry."

Still maintaining a Herculean grasp on his control, Reid asked, "Why?"

She sniffed, straightened a little in her chair, a hint of color returning to her cheeks.

"He wants me to move back to Connecticut once we're married," she answered. "But he knows my life is here now, in New York. To be close to my sisters and the business without having to commute. From the very beginning, he was fine with that—or I thought he was, anyway. He didn't even ask me to marry him until after I'd moved down here to work, and Zaccaro Fashions was up and running. He said he was proud of me, wanted my handbag designs to be successful. And that he could work anywhere. He's a lawyer," she said as an aside. "I assumed that meant he would take a job at a New York law firm and move to the city, too."

She took a deep breath, the moisture starting to dry on her face, but leaving faint streaks through the foundation of her makeup.

"Then he was offered a partnership at the firm he's with now, and everything changed. He still wants me to be his wife, but he wants me to be a proper attorney's wife. A trophy wife, I think—moving back to Connecticut to be with him, at his beck and call, giving up my work with Zaccaro Fashions to host dinner parties and attend charity events that will help further his career…"

Typical. Reid had never even met this guy, but he knew a selfish bastard when he heard about one.

"So why don't you break things off?" he suggested, hoping he didn't sound as hopeful as he felt.

Her shoulders slumped slightly and her gaze dropped to her lap. "I keep thinking…it's just a phase. That he's stressed because of his promotion. Or that maybe he's more nervous about the wedding than he lets on."

Lifting her blue eyes to meet his, she said, "He's never been like this before. I've known him for years, even before we started dating, and he's always been extremely considerate. What if he's just going through a rough patch, or dealing with something I don't understand?"

Reid clamped his teeth together so hard, he was afraid they might chip. "That's no excuse for putting your hands on a person," he bit out. "I don't care how angry you get or what the hell else is going on in your miserable, messed-up life."

She shook her head just like every other woman he'd ever met who put up with more from her significant other than she deserved.

"He didn't mean to hurt me. Not really. We were fighting and things got a little out of hand. But the minute he realized what he was doing, he stopped. I'm sure it won't happen again."

Speech number three from the Battered Woman's Handbook. And it led directly to a life of misery and abuse, and often death—either the male's or the female's, sometimes both. But try telling that to a woman in love, one who wanted to believe the best of her future husband.

So just like every third party who'd ever tried to steer an abused woman in the right direction, he said, "You don't know that. If it happened once, chances are it will happen again." After a short pause, he added, "Would you like me to talk to him?"

Kick his ass. Break his hand so he could never touch Juliet or any other person again.

"No," she responded quickly, shaking her head and sitting back in her seat. "No, no. I don't want you to do that. It was a mistake, that's all. With the wedding right around the corner, and the added pressure from our families to make it all work, everyone's nervous and emotions are running high. Everything will be fine."

She nodded, as though determined to believe her own words, even if she had to talk herself into it. Reid knew better, but also knew there was little point in arguing with her.

Pursing his lips, he waited until the red-tinged haze of anger faded from his vision. If he couldn't convince her to kick the bastard to the curb or let him track the man down and beat him to a bloody pulp, then the best he could do was offer his support. Let her know he was there for her, without judgment—none that he wouldn't tamp down and keep to himself, at any rate—in case she needed him.

Whether as someone to talk to or as personal protection once she realized her fiancé was more Mr. Hyde than Dr. Jekyll, he figured he was well qualified. She'd already confided in him, breaking down enough that he suspected she hadn't mentioned Paul's violent behavior to anyone else, including her sisters.

But he'd be even better at the personal-protection part. He was well trained and had access to a multitude of weaponry. Glancing again at the purplish bruises on her soft, pale flesh, Reid knew he would have no problem utilizing all of them. And calling in reinforcements, if he needed to.

"Where are you going from here?" he asked, catching her off guard with the sudden change of subject.

She startled slightly, giving a little sniff and swiping a knuckle delicately under each eye before licking her lips and answering, "Home."

Reid's eyes narrowed to snakelike slits. "Will the fiancé be there?"

Juliet looked even more surprised by that question. Or maybe it was simply a reaction to the barely banked fury Reid knew was still clear on his face.

"No," she replied softly. "He's on his way back to Connecticut."

"Tell you what. Just to be safe, let me take you home." Without waiting for a response, he pushed back his chair and stood.

"Oh, no, that's not necessary," she insisted, hopping to her own feet.

Rounding the desk, he took her elbow—gently, but firmly. "Please. I'll feel better knowing you got home safely."

She seemed to consider that for a moment, then on a gentle exhalation of breath, she nodded.

Opening the door, he let her pass before pulling it closed behind them. As a safety precaution, he kept his office locked whenever he was away. He trusted his staff, but there was a lot of sensitive material inside, and it was better to be safe than sorry.

"Hey, Paula," he addressed his personal secretary as they passed her desk. "Cover for me for a few hours, would you, please? I'm going to see Ms. Zaccaro home."

If Paula found that at all odd, she didn't show it. Her expression remained friendly but neutral as she gave a sharp nod. "Yes, sir."

With a hand resting lightly at the small of her back, Reid led Juliet down the hall to the elevator. Neither of them spoke a word as the car carried them silently down to the ground level.

"Did you bring a car?" he asked as they crossed the lobby, their footsteps—especially the *click-click-click* of her sharp heels—echoed in the cathedral-like space.

She shook her head briskly. "Cab."

Applying gentle pressure to her spine, he steered her slightly to the left, toward the entrance to the underground garage. "We'll take mine."

Then he looked at his watch and realized it was nearly lunchtime. Maybe he could kill two birds with one stone while he was out…and finagle a bit more time with Juliet while he was at it.

"How would you feel about grabbing a bite to eat?" he asked as they reached a sleek, onyx-black Mercedes-Benz SLR McLaren. He opened the passenger's-side door for her and added, "My treat."

Juliet couldn't remember the last time she'd had Chinese carryout. There had been a time when she and her sisters had ordered in more often than anything else. Back when they'd been thick as thieves, working 24/7 to get Zaccaro Fashions off the ground. And that was after Lily had already done more than her fair share of the legwork on her own.

Once the three of them had come together, though— Lily doing the clothing line, Zoe shoes and Juliet handbags—they'd been like a bunch of sorority girls. Staying up late, walking around in pajamas all day and eating little better than rats in a restaurant Dumpster.

It was the most fun she'd ever had.

Zaccaro Fashions was much more successful now. Still not world renowned or a household name, but they were getting there. More business meant more responsibility, though, and less time for the three sisters to spend being the Three Musketeers. Or the Three Stoogettes, as they'd often joked.

Now they all tended to drift along on their own, working privately until one of their design meetings, when they compared notes and concocted future plans. Not to mention the personal lives that seemed to separate them rather than bringing them closer.

Lily had Nigel, and split her time between New York and Los Angeles, where the American branch of his family's company was located. She was even planning a trip to England to meet Nigel's parents.

Juliet had been planning her own wedding for what seemed like forever. So long, in fact, that she now understood why so many couples chose to elope. With trips back and forth to Connecticut, her mother's and soon-to-be mother-in-law's constant input and the constant feeling that she needed to have her nose buried in copies of *Modern Bride* magazine, she was surprised her sisters hadn't disowned her already.

And Zoe was off just…being Zoe. She loved working for Zaccaro Fashions. Came up with some of the sexiest shoe designs anyone had ever seen. They weren't always practical, but they sold well to people who weren't always practical, either. But she spent just as much time out on the town, hitting clubs, maintaining her reputation as the wild child that she'd become.

So now, even though the Zaccaro sisters still technically shared the loft and the attached studio space, the takeout menus that had once gotten so much use were now tucked away in a drawer in the kitchen, all but forgotten.

Yet when Reid had invited her to lunch, offering her the choice of whatever restaurant she liked between his office and the loft, she'd found herself craving Chinese instead and suggesting they pick up something to take back to the loft with them before she even realized what she was saying.

He'd looked as startled as she felt, but then shrugged and asked if she knew a good place along the way. She'd been relieved at his easy acquiescence, and more so when he'd told her to stay in the car while he ran inside to get their order.

She knew darn well he'd double-parked as an excuse to ask her to stay with the car, since there was a legitimate space only a few vehicles ahead of them. But she was in no shape to get out and deal with the world. Her makeup was smeared from her earlier crying jag, she was sure, and frankly she felt as though she might burst into tears again at any second.

She was mortified that she'd broken down in front of Reid. Broken down *only* in front of Reid, when she hadn't even confided in her sisters about Paul's recent erratic behavior.

It had been an emotional roller coaster of a day. And not the fun kind—the kind that was rusted and rickety and threatened to fly off the rails.

But she'd felt oddly safe with him. Maybe because he was a professional who'd likely heard a million stories just like hers—and worse, she was sure—over the years. Or maybe because he'd taken on Lily's case, and then hers, and had proved to be extremely honest and reliable. He might not think so, given the strange set of circumstances surrounding his association with the Zaccaro sisters, but she certainly did. Probably because she could tell how much it had chafed that he'd been forced to juggle both of them as clients, as well as the details of their respective cases.

Or maybe because there had been something about Reid McCormack from the very beginning that told her she could trust him. There was a core of integrity to him that even a blind person could see. He wore it like a suit of armor, surrounding him every minute, everywhere he went.

On the other hand, Paul's integrity was growing more questionable by the minute.

Having time to herself while Reid was inside the Chinese restaurant waiting for their food to be prepared gave her the chance to compose herself. She was no longer crying, but she noticed that her chest was still tight with apprehension, and it took a few deep, even breaths for her to truly relax.

Then there was the matter of repairing her makeup so it didn't look like she'd just come in from a rainstorm on a perfectly sunny day. Pulling down the visor and using the mirror on the back, she was relieved to see that while things were a little mussed up, they hadn't gone into Baby Jane territory.

Her mascara and eyeliner had smeared a bit, probably made worse when she'd dabbed her eyes with a tissue and the backs of her fingers. And the light dusting of powder and blush on her cheeks needed to be reapplied to look less blotchy and uneven.

She took care of all that, plus added a fresh layer of lipstick, and finally felt better by the time Reid stepped out of the restaurant carrying a large paper sack. He got in on the driver's side, then dropped the bag on her lap, where it taunted her with a mix of savory, tantalizing aromas all the way home.

A few twinges of misgiving about inviting Reid in to share a meal gnawed at her during the quiet drive. Something like this, she supposed, could be construed as intimate or improper while she was engaged to another man. Then again, it was only Chinese, not a clandestine, candlelit dinner in the shadowed alcove of an expensive restaurant. And Paul wasn't exactly at the top of her Prince Charming list at the moment, either.

Reid had been kind enough to see her home after her upset; the least she could do was let him combine his lunch hour with the good deed.

She unlocked the door and let them in, heading for the kitchen while he took a seat on the sofa and unpacked their lunch on the coffee table.

"What would you like to drink?" she asked as she moved around, collecting plates and utensils. "I'd offer you a glass of wine, but you probably don't want to drink on the job."

Reid offered her a crooked smile, popping the top on a square white carton and taking an appreciative sniff. "I think I can handle one glass of wine. Besides, it's not like I'm a cop on duty. The rest of my day is pretty light, and if I drink too much, I can always take a cab back to the office."

"So that's a yes on the wine?" she teased.

He shot her a teasing look right back. "Yes."

"Should I ask if you prefer red or white?"

"Whatever you think goes best with Chinese takeout."

She opted for a bottle of zinfandel that was already

open and added two glasses to everything else she'd already gathered.

In the living room, she lowered herself to the sofa beside him, setting out the plates and silverware and pouring the wine. Reid doled out portions of lo mein, fried rice, General Tso's chicken and crab rangoons for each of them, then grabbed a fork and leaned back into the soft cushions of the couch.

Kicking off her shoes, she folded her legs beneath her and did the same.

For long minutes, they ate in silence. Juliet honestly wasn't sure what to say, given everything that had transpired already that day, but she was enjoying the flavors of food she hadn't eaten in far too long.

"Looks like you were hungry," Reid commented, glancing at her half-empty plate. His wasn't much fuller, though, so she didn't take it personally.

Moving what was left of her food around with her fork, she said, "Yeah. I've been a little distracted lately. Probably not eating as well as I should."

To say the least. Between plans for a wedding and her confusion about her relationship with Paul, she'd been eating like a bird. Sometimes literally grabbing only a banana or a handful of granola on her way out the door.

"Lily and Zoe and I used to order Chinese when we pulled all-nighters," she told him. "I guess I didn't realize how much I've missed it."

"Well, I wouldn't exactly call Chinese takeout 'health food,' but it sure does hit the spot once in a while."

"It does," Juliet replied softly. "And this is nice. Thank you for suggesting it."

He shrugged a shoulder, took a sip of his wine. "You're the one who said we should grab Chinese and bring it back here. I just thought it looked like you could use a break, and figured getting something to eat while I was out of the office made more sense than trying to come up with an excuse for going out to lunch *again* after I get back."

Her lips lifted in a whisper of a smile, more to herself than for him. He was just being kind, and she knew it. As owner of McCormack Investigations, he could come and go as he pleased. It was a multimillion-dollar corporation, and he employed enough other investigators and support staff that the place could probably run itself for a week or two without him, let alone a few hours.

He'd offered to bring her home to be sure she was safe. He hadn't wanted her returning to her fiancé after the confession she'd made in his office. Then he'd wanted to be sure she was okay—not just physically, but emotionally, as well. He'd brought up the idea of lunch to keep her from locking herself in the loft and spending the rest of the day moping around.

He hadn't said any of that, of course, he'd simply steered her in a direction that wouldn't allow her to be alone with her jumbled thoughts or disillusionments.

Not for the first time, she wondered why she couldn't have met Reid before Paul. Of course, she'd met Paul in college, long before she'd ever moved to New York or had the need to hire a private investigator.

But suddenly—all right, maybe not so suddenly— she'd found herself thinking about Reid much more often than she thought about Paul. Pulling away from Paul because whenever they were together, Reid's face or voice would fill her head.

When Paul would reach for her, she'd stiffen, never knowing if his touch would be gentle or rough. Reid had only ever shaken her hand or touched the small of her back, and the memory of it could make her shiver. Day or night. For no reason at all or because she'd been concentrating too hard on what it might be like to have him touch her even more. A lot more, in a lot of other places, and for much less professional reasons.

She swallowed hard, lifting her wineglass to her mouth to hide it. And to buy herself a little time while her breathing returned to normal.

She was an engaged woman. She shouldn't be sitting here lusting after another man. Even if the man she was engaged to had turned into a bit of a jerk.

But since he had, and since he was on his way back to Connecticut, Paul never needed to know that she was enjoying a very impromptu, very pleasant meal with a kind, handsome business associate.

There was no harm in that. And since this was the best she'd felt in quite a long while, she was going to savor it for all it was worth.

Three

It said something about his personal life that he was in the office, working, on a Saturday, Reid McCormack thought. And that he was happy to do it.

For one thing, the place was quiet for a change. As a private and corporate investigation firm taking up five floors in the center of one of Manhattan's tallest sky-scrapers, the office was always bustling. With people, with conversations, with the ring of phones and buzzing of fax machines. Sometimes even the weekends were busy, depending on their caseloads and the number of investigators putting in overtime.

This weekend, though, he'd lucked out. The offices— or the floor where his corner office was located, at any rate—was silent as a tomb. He could hear himself think. Hell, he could hear himself breathe.

Not that that was a good thing, not today. But at least here he had paperwork to keep him busy. Reports to fill out and review. Cases to follow up on. New employee applications to consider.

Some of it he'd been putting off for a while. Some he'd had to dig deep to come up with. Either way, it would eat up his day and keep him from going home too early to an empty brownstone where the silence was not only deafening but depressing as hell. With luck, it might also help to keep his mind off the thing he was trying desperately to avoid thinking about.

With a grunt, he closed one file folder, set it aside and reached for another.

He hadn't always hated his town house. There was a time when he'd loved it. He'd bought it slightly run-down and renovated it from top to bottom until it put all of the other houses on the block of his upscale neighborhood to shame.

Then he'd taken Juliet there. It had become their secret meeting place. A clandestine lovers' nest where they'd hidden away from the world.

Now he couldn't sleep in his bed without missing the feel of her lying next to him. He couldn't walk into the kitchen without picturing her standing at the center island in one of his discarded dress shirts, pouring fresh glasses of wine or nibbling on grapes from the fruit bowl.

The memory of her voice echoed off the walls.

The scent of her perfume hung in the air.

The home he'd once loved had turned into a bitter reminder of the woman who was at this very moment walking down the aisle into the arms of another man.

The pencil in his hand snapped. He hadn't even realized he was holding the thing, and counted himself lucky it wasn't the pen from his Montblanc set or the crystal letter opener instead.

Making a concerted effort to unlock his knuckles and loosen his grip, he blew out a breath. He might not be happy about Juliet's decision, but it was hers to make. Her decision, her mistake.

And it was well past time that he put their ill-fated affair behind him and get his head back on business. He hadn't built McCormack Investigations into a multimillion-dollar corporation by letting himself be distracted. Especially by a woman, no matter how beautiful or smart or refined she might be.

For the fourth or fifth time since he'd gotten to the office, the phone rang. Not his receptionist's line or one of the others on the floor, but his direct line. Who would be calling him here, at this number, on a Saturday?

Annoyed now by more than just the ringing phone, he snatched it up and snapped, "What?"

There was a slight pause and then a deep male voice came on the line. "Mr. McCormack. It's Glenn from the front desk."

An image of the tall, wide-shouldered security guard from the building's main lobby flashed into his head, and Reid immediately regretted his short tone.

"Yes, Glenn. I'm sorry, what can I do for you?"

"There are a couple young women down here insisting they need to see you. I told them you weren't in today, but they don't seem to believe me," he added, a touch of humor tingeing the words.

"Who are they?" Reid asked.

"Lily and Zoe Zaccaro. They say they've been calling you all morning, but you didn't answer."

With a long-suffering sigh, Reid pinched the bridge of his nose. So that explained the incessant ringing of his private line. But if there was anything he *didn't* need today, especially in his current dark mood, it was these two walking blond disasters.

Okay, so maybe "disaster" was a bit harsh. He'd never even met the youngest Zaccaro sister, Zoe, though the stories he'd heard about her led him to believe she was the wildest of the three.

But Lily was the one who'd dragged him into the crazy world of the Zaccaro trio to begin with. Theft and corporate espionage and a disappearance that had turned out to be an amateur undercover investigation, and finally his introduction to Juliet.

If Lily had never walked into his office, he'd be a happier man today, that was for damn sure. She'd brought him The Case That Wouldn't End and led him straight down the path to personal misery.

He didn't say that aloud, of course, and didn't tell Glenn to send them away. Instead, he said, "Send them up" and spent the few minutes before their arrival tamping down his temper and schooling his features. When the door to his office opened and the two sisters bustled in, he was the epitome of calm professionalism.

The two women, on the other hand, were a whirlwind of yellow taffeta, blond hair and tear-streaked faces. They let out twin huffs of relief that they'd finally reached him after numerous attempts and flopped into the guest chairs directly in front of his desk.

"Thank God," Lily sighed at the same time Zoe muttered, "It's about time."

Reid's lips twitched at the younger sister's cheekiness, but he kept his expression blank.

"Ladies," he greeted them in a clipped voice.

It was the weekend, for heaven's sake. There was nothing so pressing in Lily's ongoing design theft case that they needed to show up at his office on a Saturday, and he didn't want them thinking this sort of behavior should be repeated.

And didn't they have a wedding to attend in their fluffy, over-the-top bridesmaid gowns? Their sister's wedding, to be specific.

"This is rather unorthodox. Is there something I can do for you?"

"Help!" they exclaimed at exactly the same time. They weren't twins, Reid knew, but damned if they couldn't pass as mirror images when they acted like this.

Taking the lead, Lily leaned forward slightly. "You have to help us," she said again. "I know it's a weekend. I know you've probably had it up to your eyeballs with us by now."

Boy, she'd hit the nail on the head with that one.

"But we don't know what else to do."

"About what?" he asked calmly.

"She's missing!" This from Zoe, whose eyes were wide and glistening.

Reid's own eyes narrowed. A niggle of foreboding began to tickle at the nape of his neck. "Who?"

"Juliet," Lily supplied. Her voice had evened out a bit, as though she was growing calmer now that she knew she had the ear of a private investigator. Especially one who'd had dealings with their family before.

Reid didn't know how much Juliet's sisters knew about her involvement with him. Did they know about the affair? Had Juliet confided in them? Or had they turned to him simply because of who he was and the work he'd done for them in the past?

Taking a deep breath, Lily continued. "Juliet disappeared from the church. From her wedding. We don't know what happened. She was in her gown. Her hair and makeup were done. I checked on her and told her everything was ready to go, and then she was just… gone. She never came out, even though we were all waiting for her at the back of the church."

She dropped her gaze, plucking at the folds of her fluffy yellow skirt. "I went to check on her again," Lily said softly, "but she wasn't there."

Tears lined her lower lashes as she raised her gaze to his. "There was no note, no hint of what might have happened to her."

Reid's stomach clenched. "Do you think she ran away?"

He didn't let himself hope for that, at least not on a personal level. He'd been down that road before and ended up deeply disappointed. But if she hadn't run off on her own, the other possibilities were too frightening to contemplate.

"We don't know," Lily responded.

"What about the fiancé?" He wasn't going to use the bastard's name. And God help him if the jerk had done anything to Juliet. Reid would hunt him down and rip him limb from limb.

Zoe tilted her head. "What about him?"

"Has he disappeared, too?"

Both women shook their heads.

"No. He's still at the church," Lily told him. "Or maybe he's gone to our loft or back to his hotel by now, I don't know."

A slow wave of relief washed through him. "So they didn't run off together?" he asked, just to be sure. "Maybe they decided to elope instead, and she ran home to grab an overnight bag."

Zoe snorted. "Definitely not. Not after all of the time and money that went into planning the wedding. Our parents and his would kill them."

"She's right," Lily agreed. "If they were going to do something like that, they'd have done it weeks ago."

Reid nodded, the wheels in his head whirling with other possibilities. "Do you think she was abducted in any way? Taken against her will?"

"Oh, my God!" Zoe wailed, while the tears spilled over the edge of Lily's lashes.

"We certainly hope not," she said carefully, holding it together moderately better than her younger sister. "We didn't see or hear anything, and there were no signs of a struggle. At least not that we could tell."

"No overturned furniture? A piece of her gown that might have caught on something and torn off?"

Zoe whimpered behind the hands that covered her face. They were tough questions, Reid knew, but if they wanted him to help, he had to have the answers.

"No, nothing like that," Lily replied weakly.

He inclined his head. "Provided she left of her own volition, do you have any idea why she took off or where she'd go?"

"No. Why would any woman run away on her wedding day? Away from the church after she's dressed and ready and everyone's waiting for her?"

Reid had the kernel of an idea why, but couldn't let it cloud his mind as he focused on the job at hand. Not after the way she'd done an about-face with him not so long ago.

Normally, he'd recommend that the family of a missing person call the police and file a report. In this case, however, he suspected he would have a better chance of tracking down Juliet Zaccaro on his own. He certainly had access to better resources than the authorities, as well as an edge they would never have—a previous personal relationship with the subject.

"I take it you want me to find her," he remarked.

Recovered from her earlier show of emotion, Zoe rolled her eyes at him. "We wouldn't be here otherwise."

He ignored the sharpness of her tone, responding with an edge of his own. "For real this time, right? Not like the time she asked me to find you."

He raised a brow, his comment clearly directed at Lily, who blushed.

"Yes," she answered evenly. "She really is missing, and we really do need you to find her. Please."

"I'll need more information from you and your family. Possibly permission to search your loft and access Juliet's personal areas and assorted accounts. Banking, phone, computer, et cetera."

"Of course. Anything that will help you find her."

Despite his reluctance to get more deeply involved with the Zaccaro clan or go running after a woman who had already chosen another man over him, Reid found that he couldn't deny their request.

He didn't know where Juliet was or why she'd disappeared before she could walk down the aisle, but despite his personal feelings on the topic, he wouldn't rest easy until he at least knew that she was safe.

* * *

Careful of her footing, Juliet wrapped the sides of her unbuttoned cardigan more tightly around her torso and followed the steep, uphill trail from the dock back to her family's cabin. No one had been out to the Vermont lake house for quite some time, so the path was overgrown, the boat was still in storage and the inside of the house was in need a good dusting.

As far as Juliet was concerned, that made it the perfect spot to hide out for a while. She was thinking forever, but knew realistically that she could probably only stretch it out for a few days to a week, and she'd been here two days already.

She was a coward for running away for even that long. She should have walked into that vestibule and told her family there was something she needed to confide to them, just as she should have told them when she'd called things off with Paul the first time. Should have walked to the front of the church or asked Paul to come back and speak to her, then told him she'd changed her mind—*again*.

What was it about him, about the expectations of her family, even, that made her such a pushover and chicken?

Regardless of what anyone might have thought of her actions or mind-set, she shouldn't have tucked tail and run. But darned if she could regret the decision. Even the thought of remaining in that church, in that gown, a moment longer than she had was enough to start her hyperventilating.

Never mind the idea of actually walking down the aisle. She was certain she would have passed out right there between the pews if she'd forced herself to go through with it. Or possibly thrown up on some of the guests, since an upset stomach had become her close and frequent companion.

The one thing she knew for sure was that she was going to have *a lot* of explaining to do when she got back. To everyone.

Already, her cell phone's voice-mail box was filled to overflowing. According to the call log, it had started ringing only moments after she'd fled the church. As soon as her sisters had realized she was missing, she assumed.

But even though she knew her family must be worried sick, and the frequent ringing and beeping of her phone had driven her almost batty, she hadn't bothered to check missed calls or listen to messages. She hadn't even taken the time to turn the phone off until she'd been on the road and well away from Manhattan.

Instead, she'd hurried back to the loft she shared with her sisters, ignoring the strange looks she received from random strangers for racing around in public in her full-skirted, custom-made fairy-princess bridal gown, and grabbed her phone, money and a single change of clothes. She hadn't known where she was going or how long she'd be gone, but even though she hadn't wanted to take the time to slip out of the wedding dress right then and there, she'd suspected racing around in the thing would get old fast.

She'd been on the road a couple hours before deciding to head for the lake house, partly because she knew it would be well stocked with everything from food to clothing. Reception was lousy, though, so once she finally turned off her cell, it was doubtful anyone could reach her unless they sent up smoke signals or parachuted in.

And it was only for a few days, she told herself again. Just until she cleared her head and figured out what to do…about everything.

She was panting slightly as she reached the top of the hill and the end of the path that led into the clearing surrounding the cabin. It was brighter here, and warmer with the sun shining down on the house through the break in the trees.

Shading her eyes, she followed one long side of the wraparound porch railing to the front door…and came to a screeching halt at the sight of a hunter-green Range Rover parked right behind her silver-blue BMW.

Her heart lurched. Who did it belong to? Had someone followed her, or was it a complete stranger? And if it was a stranger, had he simply happened by—hard to do when the cabin was nearly impossible to find without directions—or was he, or she, up to no good?

A dozen home invasion/hostage movie-of-the-week scenarios played through her head and she swallowed nervously, wondering if she should move forward to investigate or race back the way she'd come to hide in the woods or hike into town for help.

Before she could make a decision, she heard a creak and heavy footsteps clipped across the porch floor. Her head swiveled and she found herself staring up into the dark, dangerous eyes of Reid McCormack.

One corner of his mouth lifted in a humorless, almost feral grin. "Hey there, runaway bride."

Four

Reid knew he shouldn't, but he was enjoying the look of shocked dismay on Juliet's face.

He hadn't wanted to come here. Hadn't wanted to see her again knowing she'd been ready to walk down the aisle and marry another man. Even after calling things off once. Even after all they'd shared. And on top of it all, she'd been ready to marry a man who hadn't treated her right—at least not since Reid had met her.

But he'd promised her sisters. And yes, there was a part of him that needed to know she was okay.

Clearly, she was, so he could head back to New York now. Leave her to her own mysterious devices. Let her explain to her family why she'd run off in the first place. He'd said he'd find her, not that he'd provide an essay on the reasons behind her sudden disappearance.

Still, he didn't move from where he stood on the

porch of her family's lake house, hands gripping the railing.

She licked her lips, the tendons of her throat flexing as she swallowed. "What are you doing here?"

"Funny thing about your family," he replied sardonically. "No matter how hard I try, I can't get rid of them. You Zaccaro girls seem to think I'm your personal problem solver."

"My sisters called you?" she asked in little more than a whisper.

"No. They showed up at my office on a Saturday, less than an hour after you ran off from your own wedding. Care to explain that one?"

She threw her shoulders back, lifted her chin. "It's none of your business what I do."

True. She'd made that clear even while they were seeing each other, sneaking around and burning up the sheets behind everyone else's backs because she hadn't wanted anyone to know about their involvement. Too bad he was part rat terrier; nothing made him dig in his heels more than being told to get lost. It was what made him such an exceptional investigator.

Pushing away from the porch railing, he straightened. "Right. But since I'm here…"

He trailed off, letting her head fill with question marks over what he'd been about to say and what his intentions were. Turning on his heel, he crossed the porch and went inside, leaving her to follow.

Or not. But if she ran, on foot or by car, he would chase her down. And he'd catch her. Again.

Who did he think he was?

Juliet stood frozen in place, scared spitless and furious beyond belief both at the same time. If that was even possible.

She couldn't believe he'd found her so quickly. Although maybe she shouldn't have been surprised, given his skill set and how good she knew him to be at his job.

But even if her sisters had gone to him for help, she didn't know why he'd agreed to look for her. She'd been pretty sure he hated her, given their last interaction. The one where she'd thanked him for being so nice and showing her a good time, but told him she didn't think things would work out between them and that they shouldn't see each other anymore.

He'd always had the softest brown eyes, like melted chocolate or a big cup of cappuccino. From the first moment she'd locked gazes with him, those eyes had told her he was strong and kind and trustworthy.

Not exactly thoughts she should have been having about a man other than her fiancé, but tell that to her heart or her gut or whatever else was screaming at her louder than her IQ.

It was why she'd broken things off with Paul the first time around. Her attraction to Reid had become too overwhelming, driving her almost inexorably into his arms. She wasn't the type to carry on an affair while she was engaged to another man, though, and knew that she couldn't continue to feign interest in her upcoming nuptials when her heart was no longer in it. But once she was free to explore her feelings with Reid—and he'd been all too happy to reciprocate—the intensity had scared her.

Maybe that was why she'd run away. Not from her wedding, but from him. Gone running back to Paul, pretending her time with Reid had never happened.

Because he was a man she could all too easily fall in love with.

As far as everyone else was concerned, she'd still been promised to Paul all along.

She hadn't known how to tell her parents that she'd called off the wedding after they'd put so much time, money and emotion into planning the event. Not to mention how much they'd been looking forward to having Paul as a son-in-law.

She'd never worked up the courage to tell her sisters, either. Because then she would have had to tell them about Reid, and she hadn't quite been ready for that discussion. It wasn't that she didn't trust Lily and Zoe with the information but simply that she didn't yet know how to put her confusing, jumbled-up emotions into words.

Then things had gotten a bit too serious with Reid and begun to scare her. So what had she done? She'd tucked tail and run. Something she realized was becoming a nasty habit.

Or maybe she was just unlucky in love and would mess up any relationship she got into. In which case, why not stick with the status quo?

No one except Reid and Paul had known she'd broken the engagement, and Paul had never given up trying to get her to change her mind. He'd apologized again for losing his temper with her. Agreed that commuting back and forth between Connecticut and New York was a compromise he'd be willing to make, at least for the first few years of their marriage. And he'd assured her that if designing with her sisters was what she enjoyed, then of course he wanted her to continue her partnership in Zaccaro Fashions.

It was everything she'd ever wanted to hear from

him, and falling back into the role of his fiancée was
so easy.... Why not simply go through with it after all?

It had all made so much sense at the time.

Fate, however, seemed to be working against her.

She had turned her back on Reid with every intention of doing what everybody expected and settling
down with Paul....

Boom! The stick had turned blue and she'd discovered she was pregnant with Reid's child.

She'd run away from her wedding to avoid marrying
a man who wasn't the father of her child....

Boom! Her sisters had sent out the private-sector version of the National Guard to track her down.

She'd snuck off to her family's lake house in Vermont to hide out for a while....

Boom! The very man she'd least wanted to deal with
was the one to find her. The one she'd suddenly found
herself alone with in the wilderness.

There was a message in there somewhere. A lesson.
A cruel, cruel irony.

And no matter how much she might wish otherwise,
she didn't think Reid would be leaving any time soon.
Never mind that he'd done his job—he'd found her,
made sure she was okay. He could go back to New York
now and report as much to her family.

But he wouldn't. He would stick around and make
her just a little bit miserable first. At least if his arro-
gant, uninvited disappearance into the cabin was anything to go by.

Juliet considered staying outside. All night, if necessary. Frankly, if the keys to her BMW hadn't been on a
hook in the kitchen—oh, so far away—she would have

jumped in the car and raced at sixty or seventy miles per hour in the other direction.

With a sigh, she began to wonder if she would forever feel like running away. And if there was anywhere far enough away to truly escape the myriad problems surrounding her like quicksand.

The smart thing to do would be to face those problems head-on, but no way was she ready for that. Not yet. It was too much, happening all too fast. She still needed time to work it out for herself, let alone figuring out how to tell the rest of the world—or the few people directly involved, at least—what was going on.

Taking a deep breath, she moved the rest of the way around the house, climbing the wide plank porch steps to the front door. She didn't know what Reid wanted, exactly. Other than finding her, as her sisters had asked, he really didn't have any reason to stick around. But she knew him well enough to realize he wouldn't leave until he was darn good and ready.

So she would play along. She'd become a rather good actress over the past several months.

She would simply do the same now, until Reid tired of toying with her and decided to leave her alone. Blessedly alone.

Pulling open the screen, she stepped inside, closing the heavier wood-and-beveled-glass door behind her. Across the way, Reid stood at the kitchen island, making himself at home by pouring himself a glass of orange juice—one of the few things Juliet had picked up at the small general store in town on her way to the cabin. He took a few long swallows before returning the carton to the refrigerator.

Crossing the wide-open space of the living room

with its floor-to-ceiling windows facing the lake, she pulled out a stool and took a seat directly across from him, keeping the width of the island between them.

She had to bite her tongue to keep from asking why he was there, what he wanted from her, why he wouldn't leave. But she knew if she spoke first, she would lose what little solid ground she currently possessed. Better to remain silent and let him steer the direction of their conversation so she at least had a clue of what was going on in that labyrinthine mind of his.

The seconds ticked by. *Tick. Tock. Tick. Tock.* Then he pulled out a stool of his own and sank down as casually as though he'd lived there all his life.

That had been something else about him that attracted her. How comfortable he seemed to be, no matter his surroundings. Of course, she supposed a man like Reid had earned that right. An ex-army ranger. A self-made millionaire. He'd been everywhere, done everything.

She didn't think he was afraid of much, either. Which wasn't to say that he let his guard down. If anything, he seemed to be always on the alert, hyperaware of what was going on around him. Another trait that had made her feel safe when she was with him.

When he finally spoke, his deep voice filling the quiet, yawning space of the house, Juliet jumped.

"So…you want to tell me what's going on?"

She licked her lips, buying time while her mind raced and her pulse returned to normal. "Nothing's going on. I just needed to get away for a while."

One dark brow winged upward. "You needed to get away," he repeated. "In the middle of your wedding ceremony. Isn't that what the honeymoon is for?"

Technically, it was before the wedding, not in the middle, but she could hear the bitterness in his tone as he muttered the word *honeymoon,* so she decided not to split hairs.

Her own stomach roiled at the thought—of being married to Paul right now, of going off with him somewhere isolated and alone. He'd booked tickets to Fiji, but her first choice had been Paris. She'd wanted to tour the Louvre and take in the cutting-edge fashions, bring home ideas for her own line of handbags and anything Lily and Zoe might like to apply to their designs. Of course, Paul hadn't *really* wanted her to continue her design work, despite his assertions when he was trying to mollify her, so he'd nixed that idea in exchange for sun, sand and skimpily clad fellow vacationers.

When she didn't respond, Reid lifted the glass to his lips and said snidely, "Maybe you finally came to your senses and decided you didn't want to be that jerk-off's punching bag for the next fifty years."

"Paul never punched me," she muttered automatically, then wondered why the heck she was defending him. It seemed like rather a moot point now, and was none of Reid's business either way.

But instead of being placated, Reid's temper flared. His scowl deepened as he snapped, "*Does it matter?* He put his hands on you. He left bruises. He used his size and brute strength to bully you."

He was up and off the stool now, coming around the island to face her more fully. She was sure he didn't realize it, but he was ten times more intimidating than Paul had ever been.

His broad shoulders. His forceful manner. His dark

good looks. The thunderous expression on his face was enough to have her quaking in her boots.

The problem was, he made her quake in a good way. Quake and quiver and sigh deep inside.

He closed in on her, the crisp, clean scent of his aftershave tickling her senses and making her lean back an inch. He didn't seem to notice.

"The only time that should happen," he ground out, "is when a man does this."

And then he was grasping her shoulders, jerking her to her feet and smashing his mouth down on hers.

What the hell was he doing? Hadn't he learned his lesson where this woman was concerned?

Apparently, she was the female equivalent of sugar, nicotine or black-tar heroin: highly addictive and nearly impossible to quit.

He shouldn't be here at all. Should have turned down her sisters' pleas for help. Should have turned around and left as soon as he knew she was alive and well. And he sure as hell shouldn't have come inside, confronted her or rounded the island counter so that she was within easy reach. Because when was the last time she'd been within reach and he *hadn't* felt compelled to touch her?

Even after everything that had passed between them—and recently, it had mostly been bad—he couldn't resist her. She felt like heaven in his arms. Soft and plush against him, her gentle curves molding to his hard planes. Her warm lips giving beneath his own.

For long, drawn-out minutes, he kissed her, tasting the mint of her gum or toothpaste or whatever else. It was so easy to block out the rest of the world when he was with her. Especially when he was with her this way.

He didn't think about the job he was supposed to be doing, or the duty he owed to her sisters, or the man she'd left at the altar. He didn't even think about how she'd left him to run back to that other man or how pissed he'd been ever since.

But he couldn't kiss her forever. *More's the pity.*

Lightening the pressure of his mouth against hers, he pulled back, encouraged when he noticed that her eyes were glassy and she was out of breath. Nice to know he wasn't the only one affected any time they were in the same room together.

Relaxing his hold on her upper arms, he ran his fingers through the hair at her temple, tucking an errant strand behind her ear. Her tongue darted out to lick lips rosy and moist from his kiss, sending a jolt of electricity straight to his groin.

"You shouldn't have done that," she said in a shaky whisper.

He took a determined step back. "Why not? You're not engaged anymore. At least I think that's what it means when you run off five minutes before saying 'I do.'"

She flinched, and he almost regretted the sharpness of his comment. Almost. Then her shoulders went back, a look of determination falling across her face.

"You need to leave, Reid," she told him frankly. "I'm fine, you can see that. Go back to New York and tell my sisters as much. Let my entire family know I'm okay and just need a little time to myself. I'll be home soon."

He cocked his head. "They're going to want to know why you took off in the first place."

She shrugged in reply. "Tell them you don't know.

You were hired to find me, not explain the motives behind my actions, right?"

Touché, he thought, biting back the ghost of a grin. "They'll want to know where you are."

Her eyes narrowed, anger beginning to flash in their icy blue depths. "Well, don't tell them," she all but snapped.

"You want me to lie to them?" He continued to bait her.

"Of course not. Just tell them that I'm safe and don't want anyone knowing where I am right now. I'll be in touch after I've worked out a few things, and there's no need to worry."

"Sounds good," he said with a nod. "They might even believe it."

While she scowled at him, he moved around the island and returned to his perch on the stool. He took a casual drink of the orange juice he'd found in the refrigerator, waiting until she dropped her guard and sat down, too.

"But how do *I* know you're really okay? What if there's something more nefarious going on that you're not saying? What if I turn around and drive back to New York only to find out later that you were hurt or abducted or arrested?"

Astonished, she raised her brow. "What would I be arrested for?"

Her voice was sharp, sounding truly offended. And he knew why—no way in hell would Juliet Zaccaro ever behave in such a manner that would cause her to be arrested. He'd be surprised to discover that she'd ever even received a parking ticket.

Juliet was a by-the-book kind of woman. She didn't

speed, she didn't raise her voice and she most certainly didn't break the law. Reid would be willing to bet that the only thing she'd ever done in her life that wasn't aboveboard and filled her with guilt was…him.

It was a bitter pill to swallow, and he tightened his jaw to maintain control of his annoyance. After a moment, he forced himself to relax, remembering that he was here to check on her, not to start a fight. Which didn't mean he couldn't continue to tease her a bit.

With a shrug, he said, "I don't know why you're here or what you've been up to. Maybe you were pretending to be engaged to that guy so you could embezzle money from him, and now you're running off to meet your real boyfriend."

Rather than shrieking like a banshee as he'd half expected, she shot him a withering glare.

He shrugged it off. "Or maybe you're a closet nudist and came up here so you could commune with nature au naturel without anyone seeing or recognizing you."

She continued to glare at him, but he didn't miss the tremor of amusement that tugged at the corners of her mouth.

"I think it would be best if I stuck around for a while, just to make sure everything's copacetic."

At that, her eyes went silver-dollar round and her mouth dropped open like a carp's.

"Oh, no. No, no." She jumped off her stool as though it had suddenly turned into a high-temperature hot plate. "Absolutely not!"

Ignoring her outburst, he slid off his own stool and started wandering around the rest of the house like a potential buyer. It was roomy and expansive, a "cabin" only in the sense that it was finished almost completely in polished oak—the floors, walls and exposed beams far overhead—and furnished in dark, woodsy colors. Millionaire rustic, for those whose idea of "roughing it" was leaving their gold card at home.

Not that he had room to judge. If he didn't work so much and had the time to get away, he'd probably build or buy a place just like this. He could certainly afford it, but along with the idea of purchasing a yacht and sailing around the world or retiring to a chateau in the Swiss Alps to spend the rest of his life skiing, it remained on his "one of these days" list.

He wouldn't mind sticking around here for a while, though. It would almost be a vacation, if he didn't count the woman who was even now staring daggers at his back.

"You're not staying here, Reid."

He didn't respond, instead glancing up at the loft visible from the living area before trailing toward a hall off the kitchen that he suspected would lead to more bedrooms.

"I mean it," Juliet continued, following behind with her arms tucked angrily across her chest.

He stuck his head into the doorway of a luxury bath—sunken tub, separate oversize shower stall, marble vanity surrounding two basins with polished brass fixtures.

"Why not? There's plenty of space," he told her without turning in her direction. She continued to follow.

"Because I don't want you here," she stressed.

After checking out another room—a nice master bedroom with attached bath, a few of Juliet's things already spread on the dressers and near the bed—he faced her.

"We don't always get what we want," he said quietly.

He watched his meaning sink in and her features go taut. She took a step back until she was pressed against the hall wall. Fighting a smile, he brushed past, returning the way they'd come.

"Fine," she called after him. "Then you stay, and I'll go."

He was in the kitchen again, her footsteps echoing as she moved toward him. He waited until she stopped before turning to meet her gaze. She looked nervous and uncertain, though she was obviously aiming for tough and unwavering.

Lowering his tone, he leaned in until he was sure she saw the gravity in his own eyes.

"Do, and I'll follow you. Doesn't matter where you go or how hard you try to get lost in the crowd, I will find you."

Five

Juliet couldn't decide whether she was more angry or frustrated. Annoyed or…oddly touched. Not only that her sisters had been worried enough about her to send Reid after her, but that she meant enough to Reid that he was refusing to leave her alone, even though he knew she was perfectly fine at her family's lake house.

Oh, it was a completely heavy-handed move on his part, which was maddening. He knew that sticking around would drive her batty, and that was exactly why he was doing it.

But beneath that was a thread of honest concern and the need to be *sure* she was all right. She'd told him as much half a dozen times, but Reid wasn't one to take anybody's word over facts and his own observations.

If she'd been anyone else, he probably would have accepted her assertion. Once he'd seen that his quarry was alive and well, and he'd been assured of her safety and location, he most likely would have turned around and headed back to New York to inform his clients of his findings.

But she wasn't anyone else. They had history together: a strange, complicated, wonderful yet awful history.

Her time with him had been some of the best of her life, but even as it had been happening, she'd known it was something that was burning too hot and fast to last.

Reid hadn't been happy about that at all.

She'd warned him from the beginning that it was just a fling. It couldn't get serious.

She'd been engaged to another man the first time she'd gotten swept up in passion and fallen into bed with him. And though she'd broken off the engagement immediately—so that she could continue to see Reid without being weighed down by suffocating guilt—she hadn't wanted anyone to know about him.

Hadn't wanted them to know she'd strayed from her fiancé. Hadn't wanted them to know she was seeing one man when she should have been planning her wedding to another. Hadn't wanted to see her parents' disappointed faces or hear the lectures about how lucky she'd been to be engaged to Paul, who came from such an upstanding and influential family.

And even if she hadn't wanted to keep her relationship with Reid a secret, he certainly wasn't looking for anything permanent. Their affair had been wild and forbidden, and completely out of character for her.

Juliet suspected that was another reason he insisted on sticking to her like double-sided tape. Unfinished business, in his mind. Not to mention a badly bruised male ego.

Which wasn't her fault. She'd been honest with him from the start. But apparently women weren't the only ones capable of getting attached and letting their emotions overrule their common sense.

She gave a snort of derision, hunching her shoulders and doing her best to snuggle more deeply into her sweater because she refused to go back inside while Reid was using the kitchen as though he owned it.

He'd insisted on fixing dinner—he said to thank her for her hospitality. Sarcasm alert on that one. It had fairly dripped from his tongue and glittered off the pearly white teeth he flashed in a wolfish smile.

She suspected his offer was based more on the fact that she couldn't cook. Well, not much, anyway. And he probably didn't want to risk food poisoning so far from town and the nearest hospital.

The good news was that whatever morning sickness she'd been suffering did tend to limit itself to the mornings.

The bad news was that sitting across from Reid right now while they shared a meal was likely to knot her stomach in an entirely different manner.

And what exactly was she supposed to do in the morning when her pregnancy symptoms did make an appearance? Every day, she tended to spend a few hours, at least, looking like an extra in one of those deadly virus outbreak movies: all sweaty and flushed and lurching around like a zombie between bouts of retching.

Oh, yes, it was lovely. She was still waiting for the part where pregnancy was a beautiful experience and she started to "glow."

She'd also heard pregnant women were supposed to

avoid undue stress, but she couldn't think of anything more stressful than being this close to Reid right now. Not after the way they'd parted, how she'd just left her fiancé at the altar and given the fact that Reid had no idea she was pregnant with his child.

She wasn't sure she *wanted* him to know, and figuring that out while he was doing his best impression of "Me and My Shadow" didn't help matters. It was going to be like counting to one thousand while someone else called out random numbers in your ear. She was starting to get a headache just thinking about it.

Another shiver stole over her and she curled her chilly fingers into fists. She really should go in before she caught a cold or turned into a human freezer pop. Only sheer stubbornness kept her outside when she knew the house was toasty warm even without a fire in the hearth.

Coming to her rescue—or perhaps luring her farther down the rabbit hole—Reid opened the front door and stuck his head out.

"Dinner's ready," he said, then disappeared back inside.

She toyed with the idea of ignoring him, just as she'd been toying with the idea of climbing into her BMW and driving away, regardless of his threat to chase after her. But in the end, she was simply too cold, too hungry, and edging toward too darn tired to fight it—*him*—anymore.

Warmth surrounded her the minute she stepped inside and closed the door behind her, chasing away any trace of chill lake air that had trailed in with her. She released a sigh of relief, rubbing her hands together before shrugging out of her sweater and draping it neatly over the back of a chair.

Then she turned her attention to the dining room table, where Reid had put out two place settings and even moved a small vase of artificial flowers from elsewhere in the cabin to the middle of the table as a centerpiece. If she hadn't been so upset with him, she might have found the scene almost romantic.

Without sparing her a glance, Reid moved between the kitchen and dining areas to fill their plates and pour a couple glasses of wine. Clearly, he'd discovered her father's collection.

Juliet's nerves began to jump as she wondered exactly how she would manage to avoid drinking the stuff after it had already been poured. Especially when she'd never been one to turn down an offer of wine in Reid's presence before.

For that matter, she was also a little bit concerned about the food scents that were mingling to fill nearly every nook and cranny of the spacious cabin. If they started to make her sick, she would have nowhere to go to get away from them and nowhere to hide from Reid's too-keen scrutiny.

So far, though, she seemed okay. She couldn't quite identify the fragrances assailing her at the moment, but they were rich and pleasant, and actually had her stomach rumbling rather than revolting.

Taking a tentative step forward, she slipped her fingers into the front pockets of her casual navy slacks.

"What are we having?" she asked as Reid took one last trip from the kitchen and deposited a platter of rolls on the table.

He lifted his head to look at her, and she pretended

not to notice the flash of heat reflected in his chocolate brown eyes. She pretended not to feel it, either, as it filled her and seeped into all of the dark, forbidden places that missed him most in the wee small hours of the night when she sometimes couldn't sleep.

"You've got a really well-stocked pantry here," he said, pulling out a chair and waiting for her to take her seat. "Not to mention the freezer and fresh stuff you picked up on the way."

Rounding the table, he took his own seat straight across from her. "I found some beef medallions and a jar of sauce, and even some frozen bread dough for rolls. The only thing we're missing is a spring lettuce salad with raspberry vinaigrette."

He smiled at her, and she couldn't help shaking her head.

"I can't believe you cook," she admitted honestly. It didn't seem like something a man like him would stoop to.

She happened to know that he was personally worth well over twenty-five million dollars. And his company, which was one of the most successful, high-tech investigation firms in the country, was worth probably closer to a billion.

But unlike Paul, who liked to brag about his financial success and spend money on expensive items that would impress his peers whether or not he needed or even truly wanted them, one would never be able to peg the size of Reid's bank account just by looking at him.

She'd seen him in a perfectly tailored Armani suit and wondered why they bothered ever using anyone else on a cover of *GQ*. She'd even seen him in a tuxedo once and thought he made every James Bond ever to grace the silver screen look like a hunchbacked, bridge-dwelling troll in comparison. So without a doubt, he could flaunt his wealth and prestige.

More often than not, though, he preferred slacks and a plain white dress shirt. Sometimes with a suit jacket. Often with a tie that didn't make it much past noon.

Even now, he was dressed in his usual business casual, sleeves rolled up to his elbows. The style wasn't fancy, wasn't expensive. She knew he had pricey clothes in his closet, but doubted he spent much on his everyday attire.

Yet it didn't take away one iota from the man she knew him to be. The one who'd spent time in the military, become highly trained, then started his own investigation firm where he could use his brains as well as his brawn.

Which was yet another reason she knew she would never manage to get away from him if he didn't want to let her go. He would use the resources of his company, his own personal skills and finally his own unlimited finances, if necessary, to track her down without ever bothering to bill her sisters for the time and money he actually spent. He was that stubborn, that persistent and apparently still that determined to make her suffer.

Luckily, just being in the same room with him for any length of time these days was enough to achieve that.

Then again, dinner looked and smelled delicious, so it wasn't *all* that bad.

She picked up her fork and knife, but waited, not wanting to be the first to begin eating. Grabbing his own utensils, Reid inclined his head, gesturing for her to dig in.

"My mother used to tell me that nothing impressed a woman more than a man who can cook," he said, cutting into his meal. "So I let her teach me, then learned a few more things on my own along the way."

"And did it work?" she asked.

He popped a piece of meat into his mouth, chewing for a minute before he replied.

"I don't know," he said, lips quaking. "Are you impressed?"

It pained her to admit it, to even be bantering so comfortably with him when there were vital issues lying just beneath the surface, but she found herself smiling in return and saying, "Actually, I am."

"Then it worked."

He took another bite, as did she, and for a while they ate in companionable silence.

"Why didn't you ever cook while we were…" She stopped midsentence, not entirely sure of what she meant to say. *While we were together? While we were having our torrid affair?*

A stony mask fell over Reid's features, but otherwise he didn't react to her blunder.

"There never seemed to be time," he responded instead. "We always seemed to be in a rush when we got together and fell right into…other things. Or we met somewhere without a kitchen that we wouldn't have bothered using anyway because we were always too busy…with other things."

His innuendos couldn't have been clearer if he'd drawn a picture on his cloth napkin, and her face flamed at the memories, as well as his suggestive tone.

"Besides, you always seemed to want takeout or delivery. Not my favorite, but it made you happy." He shrugged one broad shoulder, gaze turned down to his plate while he cut another slice of beef medallion. "And it gave us more time to do what we did best."

That was why she didn't want him here. There was too much history between them that he wasn't the least bit shy about bringing up. Something she suspected he would do quite often, both to needle her and remind her of what they'd had together. What she'd been missing ever since she'd left him and ended up right back where she'd been to begin with, engaged and planning her wedding.

He also knew her far too well. She remembered how he used to watch her from beneath those hooded lashes, studying her every move. He was a detective; he profiled people for a living.

She might be able to fool him for a while, but eventually he'd figure out that she was acting off. That there was more going on than simply cold feet and the decision not to go through with a wedding she'd been second-guessing all along. To steal a line from her British soon-to-be brother-in-law, he was too bloody smart that way.

Glancing down to avoid the flesh-and-blood reminder of just what a fix she was in, she saw that her plate was nearly empty. She hadn't realized how hungry she truly was after babying her stomach with saltines and weak sweet tea for so long.

Reid's meal, however, was hearty and appetizing, with no components that aggravated her delicate stomach. She felt like she should thank him, but since she was still fostering a good mad at him, she kept her mouth shut on that count.

Desperate to change the subject and get as far away

from "other things" as possible, she wiped her mouth with her napkin, then sat back in her chair and asked, "So how exactly did you find me? I mean, I know that's what you do, but *specifically* how did you find me?"

Reid, too, had cleaned his plate. He scraped up what little was left and took a final bite before leaning away from the table and meeting her gaze.

"GPS in your cell phone."

Her eyes narrowed. "There's no reception up here. I turned my phone off before I even arrived."

One side of his mouth twitched, and she could have sworn he was smirking at her.

"Yes, but you had it on when you left the city and for a while after. I tracked your last few locations, then did a search and discovered that your family owned property not too far from those pings."

Fine. Maybe he'd earned the right to smirk.

"But what if I hadn't been here? What if I'd changed my mind and gone on to Las Vegas or Canada or Mexico?"

He raised a brow as if to say "O ye of little faith."

"Then it might have taken me a couple more days, but I still would have found you."

That same shiver of awareness stole over her. The one that made her feel like a damsel in distress finally rescued by her strong, conquering knight in shining armor.

No doubt Reid was the strong and conquering type. As well as possessive. But none of those traits had ever been overwhelming. He'd never made her feel small or weak, controlled or manipulated. He'd only made her feel safe. Safe from harm, safe inside her own skin, safe to be herself around him.

With everybody else lately, she seemed to be playing a role. Pretending to be happy. Pretending to be excited about her upcoming nuptials and content in her relationship with Paul.

And she didn't have to pretend only around Paul or her parents, but around her sisters, too, which was probably the hardest part of all. She knew they would be completely supportive if she told them the truth, confided in them about what had been going on with Paul—the growing animosity and on-again, off-again engagement—and how close she'd become to Reid.

But for some reason, she just couldn't. It was still all a jumbled-up mess in her head. If *she* couldn't make sense of it, how in heaven's name would they?

"Well, I hope it's clear to everyone—once you tell them where I am, of course—that I wasn't really running away. I just needed some time to myself. Otherwise I really would have gone to one of those other places. Far, far away, maybe even overseas."

For some reason, it was important to her that people understood that. It made her somehow less of a coward. She hoped. Less of a horrible, despicable bridezilla/runaway bride for humiliating Paul the way she had.

Reid reached for his wine. His eyes darted to her still-full glass, and she held her breath, waiting for the inevitable inquisition that was to come. But he merely took a sip of his own Bordeaux before returning the glass to the table.

"I already talked to them. And I told them as much."

Juliet sat forward as though her chair were an ejector seat. "You talked to them? Who? Lily and Zoe or my parents? Or Paul? What did you tell them? What did they say? *How* did you talk to them? There's no reception up here."

She said the last with suspicious, narrowed eyes, and Reid had the gall to grin at her. It was enough to make her want to pick up the flower centerpiece and launch it at his head.

"Don't worry, I didn't tell them exactly where you were. I spoke with Lily and reminded her that she hadn't wanted anyone to know where she was when she ran off to Los Angeles, so she understood. I simply assured them that I'd located you, made sure you were all right and that I was also going to stick around awhile to make sure you stayed that way."

"They were okay with that?" Juliet wanted to know, still doubtful.

"I'm extremely reliable," he responded with only a hint of offense in his tone. "Besides, I promised to call again if anything changed and keep them updated on the situation."

She supposed she should be grateful but only managed to purse her lips.

He reached for his wine again. "Oh, and I've got a satellite phone. That's how I reached them when your phone wouldn't."

Behind her tight lips, she clenched her teeth. The man was so incredibly infuriating.

"Are you ever *not* three steps ahead and prepared for every eventuality?" she ground out.

She was supposed to be the squared-away one. The Girl Scout who was always prepared, always did the right thing, always adhered to proper rules and regulations and never had a hair or a button out of place. And in her family, she was. Her sisters didn't tease her about being a Miss Goody Two-Shoes for nothing.

But compared to Reid, she felt like some slovenly, disorganized mental patient. Maybe because *he* was the one driving her eight shades of crazy half the time.

Lifting the wine to his mouth, he took a long, leisurely drink, then lowered the glass and flashed her a too-confident-for-his-own-good grin. "Nope."

Six

Juliet closed the door to her room behind her, making sure it was locked. She wasn't afraid of Reid, not physically, at any rate. But she certainly didn't want him walking in on her without warning. It was all she could do to be in the same house with him without jumping out of her skin.

As soon as dinner was over and she didn't think it would be completely rude, she'd pled exhaustion and escaped his company as quickly as possible. Not that it was a lie; it had been a long, stressful day, and the pregnancy only added to her need for frequent rest. But it was late enough that she could stay in her room until morning without letting Reid know she was trying to avoid him.

With a sigh, she pushed away from where she'd been leaning with her back against the door and crossed the spacious master bedroom. When they visited the lake as a family, her parents took this room, of course. And she and her sisters took turns with the others, or would sometimes pile all together in the loft like they had when they were young.

Now, though, she was glad she'd opted for the large room with the connected bath; otherwise she would have had to risk running into Reid every time she wanted to use the bathroom down the hall.

Kicking off her shoes, she padded across the carpeted floor, stripping as she went and leaving her clothes in a pile near the closet. She would pick them up later, folding them or tossing them into the hamper, but it would probably surprise a lot of people to see that she wasn't *always* neat and almost pathologically organized. Sometimes when she was alone, she was downright messy. For short spans of time. Then her need for order would kick in and she'd run around tidying up again.

For now, however, her things were fine where they were. All she wanted was a hot shower and a comfortable pair of pajamas. Her mouth watered for that big glass of wine she'd left untouched during dinner, but she supposed she would have to learn to unwind and relax without that sort of thing for the next several months.

Feeling much better after her shower, she wrapped her wet hair in a towel and climbed into a pair of soft flannel pajamas. Thank goodness that when she'd stopped at the loft to grab a few things, she'd opted for nightclothes that were both warm and all encompassing.

The flannels were a cute, girly, pink-and-green plaid with satin accents and a feminine cut, but they covered her from neck to ankle. Just about anything else from her dresser at home fell into the nightie category and would have bared her shoulders, legs and possibly a hint of bottom curve. All body parts she wasn't keen on sharing with Reid this visit.

Back in the bedroom, she moved to the closet and picked up the clothes she'd discarded earlier, folding them and setting them aside. Inside the closet, she knew what she would find. She'd avoided looking at it since she'd stuffed it in there, but decided now that she could. She was strong enough and she was ready.

As she peeled open the louvered doors, yards and yards of taffeta and lace filled her vision. Snow-white and so beautiful, it continued to take her breath away no matter how many times she saw it.

There were a few smudges on it now that Lily would kill her for if they didn't come out. Her sister had put so much time and love into the gown. Time she could have been spending on designs for her line. But she'd been so excited about Juliet's wedding, she'd wanted her to have a truly spectacular, one-of-a-kind dress to wear down the aisle.

It wouldn't do, Lily had said more than once, for one of the Zaccaro sisters to wear off-the-rack or another designer label to her own wedding. Not when she could look beyond fabulous and maybe get them a little more exposure for Zaccaro Fashions at the same time.

Instead, Juliet had run off before anyone could see what amazing work Lily was capable of, and worn the fairy-tale gown halfway to Vermont before stopping to change into street clothes in a convenience-store bathroom.

Yeah, she might have to keep *that* part to herself, or Lily really would kill her.

Leaving the closet doors open, Juliet backed up to

the bed and sat carefully on the edge, simply staring at the gown for several long minutes.

She'd already decided she wouldn't be marrying Paul. Ever. At some point, she would have to face him again, to apologize and explain why she'd abandoned him at the altar after assuring him she really did want to go through with the wedding, even though she'd called it off only weeks earlier. With luck, it would be in a nice, crowded public place with lots of witnesses so he would be less likely to create a scene.

So wearing the gown for a second shot with him was out of the question. And if she ever, *ever* decided to give the whole engagement/wedding/till-death-do-us-part thing a try with another man—the image of Reid in a tuxedo, waiting for her at the end of the aisle burst across her brain, but she quickly snuffed it out—she didn't know if she would recycle this dress or choose another that had no old memories and emotions attached to it.

But she hated to think about it going to waste. Just hanging there in her closet forever like a forgotten prom gown, or shipped off to Goodwill where someone would pay twenty dollars for it and never know what a true treasure they'd been lucky enough to find.

Hopping up, she hurried over to the overnight bag she'd stuffed full of items she thought she might need while she was hiding out for her little breakdown-slash-journey to self-discovery and grabbed the sketch pad and pack of pencils she'd brought along. She almost never left home without them, even in the middle of a crisis.

Smiling to herself, she carried them back to the bed where she sat cross-legged, still facing the Wedding

Dress of Doom. Even at the worst of times, she was a designer at heart. She'd grabbed these supplies first and packed other things like underwear and her toothbrush second. A girl had to have her priorities.

It had been ages since she'd really had the time to work the way she liked to. The way she should have been. Lily and Zoe had definitely been carrying the weight of the company these past few months while she focused on wedding preparations and letting herself be distracted by Paul's bad behavior and her completely inappropriate yet irresistible attraction to Reid.

There was still plenty going on to distract her, but she felt oddly rejuvenated creatively. Eager to get back to work because maybe, just maybe, sketching would help to keep her mind off the problems hanging over her head. She might even manage that most coveted form of problem solving—the brilliant revelation that came out of the blue while one was focused on something entirely unrelated.

So what if she took this wedding-gown dilemma and turned it into a solution? A jumping-off point for some gorgeous new handbags that Lily and Zoe would both proclaim were well worth her minor emotional meltdown and sudden disappearing act.

Her parents might not agree, since they were the ones who were going to lose all the money they'd put into the wedding plans, but maybe the fact that she would soon be giving them their first grandchild would soften that blow.

Charcoal and colored pencils spread out beside her, she began to doodle. Just shapes and squiggly lines at first, a few that looked a bit like flowers. Then, as more solid, structured designs came into her head, the rest of her mind drifted. A left brain/right brain thing allowed her to work with focused intent while also humming one of her favorite songs, lyrics and all.

The only problem was, the song she started to sing—the one she couldn't get out of her head no matter how many other tunes she *tried* to hum instead—made her think of Reid and the first time she'd spent the night with him.

This was the third time he'd brought Chinese. It was becoming a guilty pleasure. He'd call her or she'd call him. Her sisters would be away, leaving her alone in the loft, or he would tell her to come to his place; he'd leave the door unlocked for her. These secret rendez-vous made her feel both naughty and vibrantly alive at the same time.

She shouldn't be doing it. Should have put a stop to this crazy infatuation after that first time, when she'd known things could so easily get carried away.

But they meant too much to her. She could talk to Reid in a way she couldn't with anyone else, because he knew things about her life that she hadn't shared with anyone else, and she looked forward to their casual get-togethers far too much, feeling as though they were almost the only time she could breathe easily and be herself.

Because of that, she couldn't stop. Not yet.

Besides, it was just dinner. And takeout, at that, not some romantic, candlelit meal at an upscale French restaurant. Just a carton of sweet-and-sour chicken, a couple glasses of wine and some comfortable, friendly conversation that was about something other than the wedding or Zaccaro Fashions.

Reid arrived with a firm knock, and butterflies she definitely shouldn't have been feeling unfurled in her belly, spreading to all of her other extremities.

As soon as she opened the door, he looked her up and down, his gaze raking over her like a touch. Warmth enveloped her, turning her feverish in an instant.

Maybe she was actually coming down with something. Because having this sort of reaction to Reid was wrong and not typical of her at all. She was normally so levelheaded, so steadfast. Yet being near Reid Mc-Cormack made her feel anything but.

Smiling as he brushed past, he moved to the sofa in the middle of the room and sank down, unloading the paper sack one white-and-red container at a time. Juliet collected utensils and the wine before joining him.

It was the most natural thing in the world, settling beside him. Except for the little shocks of electricity zinging through her bloodstream and raising every hair on her body. Which only intensified when their knees touched.

The breath caught in her chest, making it hard to swallow. She only hoped he didn't notice the tremor of her fingers as she poured their wine.

In an effort to get herself under control, she closed her eyes and inhaled slowly, then let the air out again as her lashes fluttered open. Reid was mere inches away, staring at her intently, and the oxygen got trapped in her lungs all over again.

"How about some music?" he asked suddenly, catching her off guard.

Before she had a chance to reply, he got up from the sofa and moved unerringly to the table in front of the windows that overlooked the street below. Along with a number of other random items she and her sisters kept there was an iPod and a dock with speakers.

The only problem was, it was Zoe's iPod. That didn't bode well for Reid finding a song that wouldn't split their eardrums or send them into seizures, since Zoe's current tastes tended toward psychedelic club beats.

To Juliet's surprise, though, he did some searching of her sister's playlists and came up with a beautiful, classical instrumental piece that filled the loft with romantic calm.

The calm part was good and much appreciated.

The romantic, she was afraid would be her downfall.

Reid returned to the sofa, and for the next thirty minutes they made small talk while they ate. Well, he made small talk. Juliet mostly nodded or offered short answers when appropriate.

She felt like a plastic doll, stiff and only able to move when someone stood behind her and lifted her limbs one by one.

Could he tell how uncomfortable she was? Or that she was only uncomfortable because she was *too* comfortable around him?

She could barely swallow the bites of food she put in her mouth and forced herself to chew, because what she wanted to do after they finished eating was lean into him and curl up at his side with her arms wrapped tightly around him.

"Finished?" Reid asked suddenly, jarring her from her wayward thoughts.

She looked down at her plate, realizing it was mostly empty. Only a small amount of rice and vegetables remained, but she knew without a doubt that she wouldn't be able to get the rest down, no matter how hard she tried.

She put her fork down across the plate, which he took from her and set on the coffee table. Then he pushed to his feet and held a hand out to her.

"Let's dance."

Juliet's heart sputtered in her chest as duty warred with desire. Oh, how she wanted to, even though she knew she shouldn't.

But he didn't give her a choice. Reaching down, he grasped her fingers and hauled her up. She went into his arms like water flowing in a stream—smooth and easy, the most natural thing in the world.

For the span of a single breath, he held her there, firm against the solid wall of his chest. The warmth of his skin permeated his pressed white dress shirt and her satin dress, and nestled deep inside her, where she hadn't even realized she was cold. It was lovely.

She nearly closed her eyes and sank even closer to him, wanting the moment to last forever. But then he stepped back, just a whisper, and she was dragged from the enchanting yet imaginary cocoon.

Tugging her around the end of the sofa, he pulled her into the large open space near the windows. The sun was going down, turning the light outside to a smoky gray with hints of orange and lavender.

Music spilled from Zoe's iPod, the beautiful strains putting Juliet in mind of long, flowing gowns, tailored black tuxedoes and a ballroom full of couples moving about the dance floor in perfect synchronicity.

Pulling her back against his chest, Reid wrapped one arm firmly around her waist while folding his other hand over hers. Almost of their own volition, the fingers of her free hand trailed upward to his shoulder, where she rested them lightly and tried to ignore the pinpricks of sensation that heated the pads of each digit before soaking into her skin and spreading through her veins.

He started swaying to the music, holding her tight, pressing his cheek to her temple. Juliet let her eyes slide closed, taking a deep, shuddering breath and then letting it out again on a sigh.

"Where are your sisters?" he whispered just above her ear.

It took her a moment to find her voice…and the will to speak at all.

"Zoe is closing up the store, then going out clubbing with her friends," she told him. "And Lily is in Los Angeles with Nigel."

"So you've got the place to yourself tonight, huh? No chance of being interrupted?"

She swallowed hard and gave a small shake of her head.

"Good," he murmured.

Then, before she knew what he was doing, he tipped her head back and lowered his mouth to hers.

His lips were warm. Salty from the Chinese they'd shared but sweet from the wine. And, man, did he know how to kiss.

He possessed her, took from her, but gave her oh, so much in return. At first the pressure of his mouth was light, testing. But once he knew she wasn't going to push him away, he delved deeper. The pressure of his lips against hers grew, and with one quick swipe of his tongue along the seam, he beckoned her to open, to let him in.

And she was powerless to refuse. She'd wanted him—wanted this—for too long.

The music swelled through the room, filling her head, sending shivers along her arms and down her spine. Or maybe that was Reid. His touch, his kiss, the anticipation of what was to come.

His hands were stroking her from her shoulders down her arms to her wrists. Her waist down to her hips, then up again over the length of her back. Her own hands simply clutched his wide shoulders, afraid that if she let go, she would slide to a puddle at his feet.

Dragging his mouth from hers, Reid continued to nibble at her jaw, moving assuredly toward the lobe of her ear. She moaned at the loss of his kiss, then again as he suckled a particularly sensitive spot on her neck.

"If we do this," he said softly against her skin, "are you going to hate yourself in the morning?"

"Probably," she admitted truthfully. Though right this minute, she wasn't sure she cared.

"Are you going to hate me?"

At that, her eyes snapped open. Her head cleared, maybe because he'd stopped nuzzling her throat, her cheek, just behind her ear. He was watching her now, his brown eyes gone dark, his gaze intensely serious.

He was waiting for her answer, and the entire direction of the rest of the evening depended on it.

"No," she told him. Simply. Honestly.

She could never hate him, no matter what passed between them. No matter how much guilt it might leave her to carry around for the rest of her life.

Whatever happened—here, tonight, with him—would be on her and her alone. And heaven help her, she wanted it. She wanted to be here with him, to be with him the way she'd imagined so many times, for so long.

Anything else, she pushed to the back of her mind. Far, far away from Reid's hands on her body, his gaze on her face, his mouth promising untold pleasures.

"Good."

He drove his fingers into her hair, cupping her head and holding her in place while he ravished her mouth. Her own hands came up under his arms to clutch his back, fisting the fabric of his shirt.

For long minutes, he kissed her while she all but sagged in his embrace. And then he released her mouth, dropping one arm to her waist and the other behind her legs to scoop her up off the floor.

She wasn't expecting it, but it didn't surprise her, either. It felt right, and she relaxed in his hold, wanting to rest her cheek on his shoulder in true damsel-in-distress fashion.

"Which way?" he demanded, and she didn't need to ask, "To what?"

She pointed toward the stairs and he marched in that direction, taking long, determined strides. When he got to the steps, he took them two at a time. Another lift of her finger told him which room was hers, and he pushed open the door, kicking it closed behind them with the heel of his shoe.

He carried her to the bed, which was neatly made, two rows of decorative pillows looking as though they were ready for a *House Beautiful* photo shoot. Everything in her room was picture-perfect. Style and organization helped her feel more in control of the world around her.

Reid clearly didn't feel the same. Shifting her weight

in his arms but not letting go of her in the least, he reached for the pillows, tossing half of them to the floor before snagging the corner of the duvet and flicking it to the end of the bed.

Then and only then did he turn and deposit her in the center of her pressed floral sheets. They had tiny purple violets on them to match the solid purple of the coverlet and pillows, and she suddenly felt self-conscious about the overly feminine tones of the room when Reid was so very masculine. She almost expected the little violets to turn into footballs or some such from his presence alone.

But he didn't seem the least bit interested in the room's décor. He only had eyes for her, as he towered over her with one knee on the bed, his gaze burning like a bonfire.

A shiver ran through her as he reached for the top button of his shirt, muscles rippling beneath the crisp cotton. His fingers were bronze against the stark backdrop, working easily, deliberately moving in a slow line down the center of his chest.

One by one, the buttons slipped from their holes. Inch by inch, she was teased by glimpses of smooth flesh. When he reached the bottom, he tugged the tails from the waistband of his slacks and shrugged out of the shirt altogether, letting it float to the floor in a cloud of white.

Juliet swallowed hard. His chest, which she'd pictured in her mind for weeks, was now gloriously bare in front of her. Broad and well defined, it was covered with a light sprinkling of dark hair. It was obvious he worked out, stayed in shape, kept his military physique despite his current corporate vocation.

Leaning over her, he unbuckled the narrow belt at her waist, sliding it free before moving his hands to the hem of her satin dress. He pushed the material up, up, slowly upward. His warm, callused palms remained flat against her skin, raising goose bumps the entire length of her body as he skimmed them over the outside of her thighs, her waist, her chest, lifting her arms and tugging the dress off over her head.

She was left in her bra and panties. A sexy, matching set in magenta satin and lace to go with the dress Reid had just disposed of.

She swallowed hard, trying not to squirm beneath his intense scrutiny. His brown eyes smoldered like pools of molten lava as he raked her from head to toe and back again.

He started to reach for her at the same time she sat up. They met in the middle, mouths meshing, bodies pressing together.

His fingers tangled in her hair, holding her steady for his kiss while she fumbled for his belt. He grunted and gave an involuntary jerk when she hit pay dirt. Slipping the smooth leather from its buckle, she let the ends fall aside to concentrate on the front of his slacks.

By touch, she undid the top clasp and slowly lowered the tab of the zipper. He groaned as she reached inside to cup him through the thin barrier of his briefs, and she reveled in his heat and hardness, in the power of holding him at her mercy in the palm of her hand.

Or maybe she was at his mercy. Sliding his hands around her back, he unhooked her bra. The straps slumped from her shoulders and he dragged them the rest of the way down her arms, leaving her bare to the evening air and his intent gaze.

She released him long enough to shrug out of the bra entirely and drop it over the edge of the bed. Clutching his shoulders, she let him lower her back onto the mattress, but brought him with her. He snaked his fingers under the elastic band of her panties, drawing them down her legs and off. Then he sat back on his haunches.

Without taking his eyes from her, he dug into his hip pocket, removed his wallet and took out a single condom. He tossed it onto her stomach, the cool plastic on her bare skin causing a chill.

Once he had what he needed, he kicked out of the trousers altogether, dropping them to the floor with the rest of their discarded clothes. She moved the condom packet aside and raised her arms, inviting him closer.

The look in his eyes as he lowered himself against her chest and into the cradle of her thighs was wolfish to say the least. She had a brief flash of being Little Red Riding Hood, about to be devoured by his wild, furry badness. *My, what big...everything you have.*

As eager as she was—as they both were, she knew—he rested atop her gently and kissed her with soft, sweet abandon. Her breasts were pressed nearly flat between them, the nipples peaking at the slight abrasion of firm to delicate, rough to smooth.

She shifted, letting that friction heighten the sensations filling her even more, loving the weight of him sinking her farther into the mattress, the heat of him rubbing suggestively against the mound of her sex.

She stroked his back, down the line of his spine to tickle the top of his buttocks, then back up to sift through the short strands of his hair. He groaned, and she returned the sentiment with a long, drawn-out, pleasure-filled moan.

Reid rolled toward the center of the bed, bringing her with him. His hand slipped between them to cup her breast. He kneaded the mound of pillowy flesh, running the pad of his thumb across the tight tip until she wiggled in his hold, wanting closer, wanting more.

And he gave it to her. Rolling the other way, he switched hands, switched breasts, pressed his pelvis even tighter against her own. Her legs were up around his hips, canting forward, straining.

She was panting when he pulled his lips from hers, but at least she wasn't the only one. His chest rose and fell with his ragged breaths, his smooth, tanned skin glistening with a fine sheen of perspiration.

"You're killing me," he murmured raggedly, his lips trailing across her collarbone, her shoulder, the slope of her breast.

Juliet tried to laugh, but it came out nothing more than a strangled gasp. "You should be inside my skin," she managed. Barely.

What could only be described as a wicked, lascivious smile crossed his face. "I'd love to."

Searching the top of the bed for the condom, he found it stuck to her left buttock. He chuckled as he peeled it away.

"That's *not* where that goes."

"Uh-uh," she agreed, letting the sound roll from her throat. "Would you like me to show you where it *does* belong?"

The cords of his neck went taut, standing out in stark relief as he swallowed. Taking that as a yes, she snatched the plastic square from his loose fingers, tearing it open at the corner. Her own hands were trembling a bit, though, so it took her a minute to get to the thin circle of latex inside.

Finally, after struggling for so long she wanted to weep, and before Reid could yank the protection away from her in frustration and do it himself, she had the condom out and was able to cover the very tip of his straining erection.

It was hot to the touch, hard as steel, but soft as velvet at the same time. She stroked its length from the base to where the first hint of latex rested.

Reid growled low in his throat, head tipping back and nostrils flaring. "If you take too much longer with that, we're going to miss having any real fun."

This was fun, watching his features tighten as she toyed with him, delighting in the fact that she held him teetering on the edge. But she definitely wanted more. She wanted the *real* fun she knew awaited them.

Nibbling her bottom lip, she resisted the urge to explore him further and concentrated on carefully rolling the thin layer of protection into place.

Truth be told, she'd never done this before. She could count the number of men she'd been with intimately enough to require a condom on one hand, and the man she'd been with most often—Paul—tended to take care of it himself so they could get down to the perfunctory act of sex. It had been so long since she'd been with him that way, in fact, she couldn't even remember if it had ever been more than that. Passionate, desperate, necessary instead of simply predictable and obligatory.

They hadn't even gotten to the good stuff yet, and already being with Reid was heads and shoulders and arms and legs and all the naughty bits in between above anything she'd experienced with Paul.

Reid made her elbows sweat. Her toes curl. Every hair on her body stood up with static electricity just from being in the same room with him. Being naked and lying beneath him made that electricity increase in voltage about a thousand percent and zing through her bloodstream like a live wire spinning out of control.

Guilt at that thought—not to mention what she was about to do—tried to rear up, but she tamped it back down. She'd made her decision.

She knew now that she couldn't go through with a marriage to Paul. She would have to break things off with him immediately. Was beginning to wish she'd listened to the tiny voice at the back of her head that had been nagging her for weeks now and done so already.

But for now, she wanted to be with Reid. Here, now, at least once. Damn the consequences. Whatever they were, she would deal with them in the morning.

Her fingertips lingered where she'd finished covering him and he grasped her hand, moving it where he wanted. In strong, self-assured strokes, he double-checked the smoothness of the condom, making sure it was properly in place.

Then he linked his fingers with hers and, palm to palm, raised her hands over her head to lie flat on the mattress.

"Better," he murmured against the corner of her mouth, nipping her lips with his teeth. "Are you ready?"

Her entire body went taut, as though someone had threaded a string from the base of her spine to the nape of her neck and given it a sharp yank. She was *so* ready. Beyond ready. Starter-pistol-at-the-beginning-of-a-race,

just-hit-Play, melted-chocolate-fountain-just-waiting-
for-a-piece-of-succulent-fruit ready.

She did not, however, seem capable of simple speech.
Her lips parted, but nothing came out past her dry, cot-
tony tongue. She swallowed and tried to lick her lips…
for all the good it did.

Giving up, she took a deep breath, shuddering again
as the action lifted her breasts to brush the firm wall of
his chest and sensation rippled through her. She nodded.

He smiled down at her, his expression so kind and
understanding that her heart swelled. Then he kissed
one corner of her mouth, followed by the other, and finally the center, slipping his tongue inside for a long,
leisurely exploration.

Lower, he caressed her waist and hip, the inside of
her thighs. Gently, he pushed them apart, making even
more room for himself. Room to move and rub and
drive her crazy.

Still kissing her senseless, urged on by her fingers
in his hair and her nails raking his scalp, he cupped her
rear in one hand, her feminine mound in the other. She
moaned into his mouth, writhing against him, straining even more as his fingers teased her swollen folds.

She was wet with desire, growing even more so as
he tormented her relentlessly. Rubbing, kneading, mim-
icking with his hand what she wished he were already
doing with his strong, hard body.

"Reid," she panted, her voice little more than a
thready whisper. "Please."

"Done with the foreplay, huh?"

She felt his grin as he brushed the sandpaper rough-
ness of one cheek against her own.

She gave a strangled laugh. "Hours ago. I didn't need it to begin with."

"Well, why didn't you say so," he all but growled.

Bending her knees and hitching her legs at his hips, he found her slick opening with the tip of his shaft and slid inside in one slow, easy glide.

She sucked in a sharp breath and held it as his size, his heat, the fullness of his entry swamped her.

"Okay?" he asked just above her ear, his own breath sawing in and out raggedly.

In answer, she gave a long moan and tightened her legs around his waist.

He chuckled. Or attempted to, anyway. "I'll take that as a yes."

She wrapped her arms around his shoulders and pulled him even closer, arching her pelvis and giving her inner muscles an encouraging squeeze. *"Yesss."*

Reid muttered a curse, lips peeling back from his straight white teeth and eyes nearly rolling in their sockets. In the next moment, he was moving, thrusting with smooth, powerful strokes. Each time he withdrew, she wanted to whimper at the loss. Each time he filled her again, she wanted to cry out in ecstasy.

Pressure and sensation built, first flowing outward like the ripples of a pond after a pebble has been thrown in, then winding tighter and tighter like the coils of a spring. She scored his back with her nails, afraid she would leave welts but unable to control herself.

Reid's own hands seemed to be everywhere at once. He clutched her shoulders before running his palms down either side of her spine, cupping her bottom, roving back up to her waist and around to plump her breasts, plucking the nipples until every nerve in her body sat up and took notice.

For long minutes, only the sounds of their heavy, staccato breathing and their bodies moving in tandem filled the room. She thought she tasted blood from where she was biting so hard on her lower lip, her head thrown back in growing ecstasy.

She clutched at him, panting, desperate, murmuring his name over and over as she strained for what she needed. That pinnacle of pleasure only he could give her, but that he was holding just out of reach.

And then Reid's own grip on her tightened, a steel-like vise of fingers on flesh while he drove into her. Hard, fast, deep—so good it brought stars to her eyes.

Her climax, when it came, hit her like a runaway train. Out of nowhere and with enough force to bow her spine and push her into the mattress while Reid stiffened above her and pressed her down even more.

He collapsed atop her on a long, satisfied sigh. His weight blanketed her. A hot, heavy blanket that should have been smothering but instead made her feel safe, enveloped, content enough to remain this way forever.

Reid started to shift, pulling out of her and rolling to his side. A tiny part of her cried, *No, no, please not yet. Please don't let it be over just yet.*

But instead of getting up, instead of leaving her in the bed alone, he tugged her close, wrapping her arm around her and draping her across his chest.

"Hope you don't mind," he said in a dry, graveled voice near her temple, "but I'm going to stay for a while."

The part of her that had panicked a moment before

did a happy little flip-flop, grinning like a girl who'd discovered her birthday party included pony rides.

"If your sisters come home, I'll hide in the closet."

That reminder burst one of her birthday balloons. Pushing it aside, she held on to her happiness as tight as she could and responded with something she knew he would find amusing.

"Mind if I hide in there with you?"

He chuckled, the rumble of his chest vibrating beneath her cheek. "I wouldn't have it any other way."

Seven

Sitting at the kitchen island of Juliet's family lake house, Reid checked his watch for the fourth time in ten minutes. He drummed his fingers impatiently on the countertop and resisted the urge to tip his stool back on two legs like a grade-schooler.

What was taking her so long?

Granted, he didn't know the ins and outs of her daily routine—at least not as well as he might once have wanted to—but sleeping past ten o'clock in the morning seemed somewhat excessive for a woman like Juliet. She may have been born with a silver spoon in her mouth, but she'd also been raised with a strong work ethic. She and her sisters hadn't built Zaccaro Fashions into a successful design label by lying in bed all day.

Plus, he knew Juliet. She was much more put-together than that. More of the early-to-bed, early-to-rise type.

Of course, it didn't help that he'd been up since 6:00 a.m.—after a night of zero sleep. But how the hell was he supposed to rest knowing she was just across the hall? Only two thin wooden panels and a few feet of oaken floorboards away, close enough to touch.

He'd paced his room half the night, as edgy as a caged tiger, working off some of the frustration and restless energy he hadn't so much as hinted at while he'd been in the same room as Juliet. Because the last thing he wanted to do was kill time at her family's lake house when they should have been headed back to New York already. He wasn't entirely sure what would happen once they got back to the city, but turning her over to her sisters would be one huge item off his to-do list.

And that was what he wanted, right? To be done with Juliet and the whole Zaccaro clan as soon as possible.

Yet for some reason, he hadn't pressured Juliet to head back to New York last night. Hadn't tossed her over his shoulder and carried her to his Range Rover, tying her up in the backseat if necessary.

Flicking his wrist, he checked his watch again. Ten-twenty.

Enough was enough. Whatever was going to happen today, it was going to happen soon. Even if he had to throw a bucket of ice water on Sleeping Beauty to get her out of bed.

Stalking down the hallway, he lifted a fist to knock, but froze as he heard a peculiar sound on the other side of her closed bedroom door. He cocked his head, listening.

Silence.

He waited a few seconds, then raised his hand again,

but before knuckles met oak, the same sort of noise reached his ears, less muffled this time.

Frowning, he turned the knob and slowly stepped inside, looking to see if Juliet was sleeping in the bed. It was empty. The covers were rumpled, proving she *had* been there at some point, but she wasn't there now.

The strange sound came again, and his head swiveled in the direction of the master bath. What *was* that? It sounded like...

Four long strides took him to the bathroom doorway, and one glance inside showed him that he'd been right. Juliet was on the floor, curled around the commode, retching like a drunk after a weeklong bender.

"Good God. Juliet."

He reached her in the blink of an eye, going down on one knee on the cool tile floor and brushing the hair back from her face. She was ashen, her dry lips parted slightly, lashes fluttering above her pale cheeks.

"Are you all right?" he asked in a harsh whisper. Then felt like an idiot for asking such a stupid question. Clearly she was far from all right.

Though what could have happened in the past ten to twelve hours that would cause her to be this sick? She'd been fine last night, so if it was the flu, it had come on fast.

Could it be...food poisoning? They'd both eaten exactly the same things, and he was okay, but... If something he'd prepared had done this to her, he would feel horrible. Grab-a-shotgun-and-take-a-long-walk-in-the-woods horrible.

"Sweetheart," he murmured, frowning so hard it almost gave him a headache. "I'm so sorry. Here, let me help you."

She groaned and tried to swat him away, but he only brushed damp blond locks from her face before getting up and moving to the sink. Wetting a washcloth with cold water, he wrung it out, then brought it back and began to gently pat her cheeks, her brow, the back of her neck.

To his relief, she sighed and seemed to relax, as though the cool cloth was some small bit of comfort on the deserted island of her misery.

A minute, maybe two passed while he continued to bathe her face and stroke her hair. Then, without warning, she lurched forward and began throwing up again.

Reid's heart twisted in his chest. Yes, it was awful to be around someone who was this sick, and normally all he'd want was to get as far away from the puking as possible. But he couldn't leave Juliet. The thought never even crossed his mind. The only thing he wanted was to make it stop, to try to make her feel better.

As soon as the latest round of illness ended and Juliet slumped over weakly, Reid jumped up and grabbed a towel, folding it into a makeshift pillow and easing her onto the tile floor. Rewetting the washcloth, he placed it on her forehead, then said, "I'll be right back."

Taking off at a sprint, he hit the refrigerator and was back beside her again in under sixty seconds.

"Here," he murmured, sinking down in front of the tub and lifting her up beside him, into his arms. She moaned, the sound a wordless plea as he brushed his lips along her brow and popped the tab on the can of soda he'd brought back with him.

"Here," he said, holding it to her lips. "Take a sip. It will help you feel better, I promise."

She did as instructed, and he thought he heard a

small sigh of delight. He only let her have a little bit, though, pulling the can away to run its chilled aluminum surface here and there over her perspiration-damp face. She liked that, too, he could tell.

After several long minutes of sipping the clear soda and running the cold can along her cheeks and brow, she began to stir. Her lashes slowly parted and she stared up at him with fever-bright eyes. She wasn't actually that hot, though—warm from exertion, but not burning up with fever.

"Feeling better?" he asked, still brushing back her hair and patting her with the cool soda can.

She nodded, struggling to lick her lips. "What time is it?" she wanted to know, but the words came out cracked and dry.

He offered her another sip of soda, lifting his arm to glance at his watch. "A little after eleven, why?"

"I should be okay soon," she murmured, pushing herself up and away from him to lean against the side of the tub alone.

Reid popped his jaw, trying not to feel annoyed by her sudden rejection. Then he zeroed in on what she'd said.

"What do you mean you should be okay soon?"

Food poisoning or the flu or whatever other unknown virus she might have picked up wouldn't come with a scheduled end time, would it?

Leaning her head back against the edge of the tub, she let her eyes slide closed. "It usually passes by eleven or eleven-thirty."

"*What* passes by eleven or eleven-thirty?" His brows drew down, confusion and suspicion warring inside his brain.

She shook her head, essentially dismissing him as she rolled away from him and climbed none too steadily to her feet. She held on to the side of the bathtub, rested a hand on the back of the toilet, and lurched her way to the sink. Running a bit of cold water, she splashed her face and patted it dry with a nearby hand towel before smoothing her hair back into a tight ponytail and setting it in place with a band from the vanity.

Without a word, she left the bathroom on shaky Bambi legs, making Reid wonder if she was going to walk away from him on stubborn principle alone only to drop into a dead faint on the other side of the bedroom door.

On a huff of frustration, he pushed to his feet and followed her, carrying the half-empty can of soda along with him.

Sure enough, he found Juliet collapsed on her side on the bed, as though she'd made it as far as she could before her short burst of energy abandoned her and she could go no farther.

Damn obstinate woman. She would freeze to death in the Arctic before accepting a coat from someone she didn't want to speak to.

Crossing to the bed, he set the soda on the nightstand, then nudged her over a couple inches and hitched a hip on the mattress beside her. He didn't touch her, pretty sure any attention on his part right now wouldn't be welcome, but had to curl his fingers into his palm to keep from stroking her hair again or brushing his knuckles lightly across her cheek.

"Do you want to tell me what's going on?" he asked softly.

She rolled her head back and forth in response, doing her best to ignore him otherwise.

"Let me rephrase," he said a bit more firmly. "What is going on?"

With a moan, she squeezed her eyes shut even tighter, refusing to answer.

"Do you have food poisoning?" he wanted to know.

"Yes."

Too quick, which meant no. "Funny, because we ate exactly the same thing last night, and I'm fine."

A beat passed in total silence.

"Do you have the flu?"

"Yes."

Again, instant response. She was lying, but why?

"That's funny, too, because you're not all that feverish, and you were perfectly well last night. No complaints that you were feeling under the weather. And I'm okay. You'd think I'd have a few symptoms, too, if you were contagious."

He could hear crickets. Or maybe this far out, they'd be cicadas.

"So that leaves...what?" he continued when she didn't show signs of giving in. "Meningitis? Scarlet fever? Ebola? Rabies?"

"Morning sickness!" she shouted without warning, interrupting his long list of not-very-likely communicable diseases. "It's morning sickness, okay?" And then she yanked a pillow from its spot near the headboard and buried herself beneath it.

Pregnant. She was pregnant.

Reid had been shell-shocked a few times in his life— once even literally while in combat—but never before had he been struck deaf, dumb and blind as a bat all in one fell swoop.

Maybe Juliet really did have something contagious, because he was suddenly dizzy, sweaty, clammy and nauseated. It had taken every ounce of strength he could muster just to stand up and drunkenly make his way out of the master bedroom, down the hall to the great room and outside onto the porch.

He'd stood there for he didn't know how long, the sturdy wooden railing the only thing keeping him upright as his knees did some sort of gelatinous jiggle that threatened to dump him flat on his ass and he dragged giant gulps of fresh air into his lungs in an attempt to avoid doing something totally embarrassing like passing out or throwing up.

Damn it, he shouldn't be this worked up by Juliet's news. After all, it was none of his business, was it? If she wanted to get herself knocked up by her jerk of a fiancé then run away from her wedding before the bastard could make an honest woman of her, that was no concern of his.

He was only upset—and physically ill—at the thought of her having another man's baby. Especially *that* man's. Reid might never have met the guy in person, but he knew a lot more about Paul and Juliet's relationship than he would have liked. Worse, he knew how the so-called groom had treated his bride-to-be, and it was enough to make Reid see red.

And now she was tied to that son of a bitch. Forever.

Pulling himself together as best he could, he went back into the house. Juliet was nowhere to be seen, so he assumed she was still in her room. To kill time and burn off some of the angry energy prickling like needles just under his skin, he prowled the kitchen, opening and closing cupboard doors, looking for nothing in particular. He sure could use a drink, though, he thought, and wondered where her father kept the good, hard liquor.

A few minutes later, still sadly lacking the buzz of aged scotch in his bloodstream, he heard a click followed by soft footsteps coming down the hall. Turning in that direction, he straightened, taking a deep breath and steeling his spine for whatever was to come.

The first thing he noticed when Juliet came into view was that she looked a hell of a lot better than she had a little while ago. She was dressed, her face freshly washed and her hair freshly brushed, though still pulled back in a sexy, bouncy ponytail.

No, not sexy. He shouldn't—*couldn't*—be thinking stuff like that about her any longer. She looked better, that was all. Less like death warmed over.

Acting nervous and uncomfortable, she stuffed her hands into the front pockets of her tan slacks and slowly approached the marble island.

"Hey," she said, so low he barely heard her.

"Hey," he greeted in return. "Feeling better?" he asked, even though he could already tell she was.

A flush of pink washed over her high cheekbones. "Yes, thank you."

And then a thick, awkward silence fell over the room. They stood there, on opposite sides of the central countertop, and neither of them knew what the hell to say.

What Reid *did* know, however, was that he had to put this situation back on solid ground. He, especially, needed his professional footing beneath him.

No more kid gloves. No more taking it easy on her because of their history. Time to remind himself that he was on the job. *She* was a job. Just get it done and get back to the office.

"Look," he said, pushing away from the counter but keeping his hands safely curled around the edge. "I'm sorry you were sick this morning, but it's clear you're all right now. Generally speaking. I'll go back to New York and reassure your sisters that you're okay. I won't tell them where you are, just that you need a bit of time to yourself and will come home or call when you're ready."

Licking her lips, she lowered her gaze for a moment, then raised it again, her blue eyes sharp but wary.

"Aren't you going to ask me about…earlier?"

His chest hitched, and for a second he held his breath. Then he forced himself to relax, forced himself to breathe evenly.

"None of my business," he said as much for her benefit as for his own. "I assume you had your reasons for skipping out on your wedding in your condition, even though most women would be running toward the father of their child, not away from him."

He shrugged and it was his turn to shift his gaze elsewhere. He chose a spot over her right shoulder and focused on one of the etched glass cupboard doors.

"I'm sure you and your fiancé will work it out. Especially now that he's about to become a proud papa."

If the words sounded bitter, maybe it was because they were. The guy she was pregnant by was a grade-A jerk and abuser. She might have run away from her wedding—probably because she'd been shocked by the discovery of her pregnancy; the timing certainly suggested the two circumstances had overlapped. But no doubt she would run back to him soon enough rather than be an unwed expectant mother.

The fact that Juliet had been fool enough to become reengaged to him in the first place, let alone get pregnant by him, made Reid want to punch something. Hard. Paul Harris's face came to mind.

"Oh, I'm pretty sure Paul and I won't be working out anything."

His brows knit at that, but he kept his lips sewn tightly shut. Not his business. Not his business. The sooner he distanced himself, the better.

"If running away from the wedding wasn't enough to put an end to things, finding out about this baby sure as heck would be."

He gave a snort of derision. He hadn't meant to, it just sort of came out.

"And why is that? I'd think good ol' Paul would be even more eager to hustle you down the aisle now that you're pregnant with his kid. Wouldn't an illegitimate heir tarnish his sterling reputation?"

Juliet inhaled deeply, her chest rising as her lungs filled.

"That's just it," she said on a whisper of air. "It's not *his* baby. It's yours."

Eight

As bombs went, Juliet's left a mushroom cloud of stunned silence and devastation hanging over their heads.

She still didn't know why she'd done it. She'd had absolutely no intention of telling Reid about the baby, regardless of the fact that he'd shown up out of the blue and refused to leave.

But then he'd caught her puking her guts up—a delightful daily side effect of this whole pregnancy business. He'd been surprisingly sweet and concerned, she had to admit.

So even though she hadn't intended to reveal her secret to anyone so soon—least of all Reid—she'd sort of owed him an explanation for the past hour and a half of her reenactment of *The Exorcist*. And the truth was that she would have told him eventually. He had a right to know he was going to be a father, and she didn't have it in her to keep something like that from him forever.

Like ripping off a bandage, she'd decided to just blurt it out. As soon as she was dressed and presentable and able to stand upright for more than five seconds without the room spinning like a Tilt-A-Whirl.

Now, though, she was beginning to rethink her brilliant and noble idea. Because Reid didn't look as though he was handling it well at all.

As soon as the words had left her mouth, he'd gone paler than a ghost. Worse, she'd be willing to bet, than she'd looked while hunched over the toilet bowl.

He'd stared at her as though wings had sprouted out of her back and she'd flown into the rafters of the cabin. And then he'd turned on his heel and stalked out.

He was still out there, pacing the length of the porch. She could hear his heavy footfalls as he marched back and forth, back and forth. Pausing occasionally with his hands on his hips.

Through the wide front window, she saw his mouth moving and the shake of his head, and wondered what he was saying to himself. She suspected it was nothing nice, at least not where she was concerned, and likely dotted with some colorful, creative curses.

After what seemed like hours of giving him his space and time to absorb the news, Juliet released a sigh and slid off of her stool, leaving the last of her can of clear soda behind. Thank God for Reid's quick thinking and her father's habit of keeping the lake house well stocked. The soda had really helped to settle her stomach and get the morning sickness to pass a little more quickly.

Moving to the front door, she opened it quietly and stood there for a moment while Reid continued to pace.

When he reached her and saw her from the corner of his eye, he stopped, the expression he turned on her dark enough to melt glass.

A muscle in his jaw ticked, and she stiffened, almost afraid of the onslaught of whatever he was about to say. Taking a deep breath, she decided to beat him to the punch.

"Before you say anything," she said on a rush, "you need to know that I don't expect anything from you. I only told you because I believe you have the right to know, but you don't have to be involved. I'll be just fine on my own. You don't have to worry that I'll come after you for child support or anything like that."

And for the first time since the plus sign had appeared on that tiny test strip, she realized it was true. She would be just fine.

Oh, there would be some explaining to do, some "cleanup in aisle three" with her family and with Paul. But she was a strong, independent woman. She had a good job and great loved ones to fall back on. Without a doubt, she knew that once they got over the shock, they would support her unconditionally and be there for her if she needed anything along the way.

So she would be a single mother—so what? She would be a good one. She would be a great mother and have a permanent reminder of her time with Reid for the rest of her life. That would make her sad once in a while, she was sure, but for the most part it would fill her with only happy memories. Eventually.

Feeling more confident than she had in quite a while, Juliet waited for Reid's tense posture to relax. For him to blow out a relieved breath and say, "Okay, great, thanks." Because what man wanted to have an unplanned pregnancy and impending fatherhood dropped in his lap?

Of course, if he wanted to be part of his child's life, she would allow it. It would make things more complicated for her in a lot of ways, but it was only right.

Instead of the *whew* she'd anticipated, however, his glare grew even darker, the slash of his mouth flattening even more, and she could have sworn she heard his molars grinding together.

"Are you sure?"

She blinked, confused. This wasn't the direction she'd expected the conversation to take. "Excuse me?"

"Are you sure?" He bit the words out, each one exploding like gunfire in her ears. The corner of his left eye started to twitch. "Are you sure you're pregnant? And that it's mine?"

At the second part of his question, she flinched. And then straightened defensively.

"Yes. On both counts."

That muscle along his jawline jerked again.

"So you've seen a doctor," he said, making it more of a statement than a query.

"No." She wrapped her arms across her waist, caught slightly off guard. "But I took one of those over-the-counter tests, and it was positive."

Not to mention the morning sickness, missed periods and myriad other symptoms that told her the little plastic wand she'd left in the church wastebasket wasn't wrong.

Reid's teeth were clenched, his eyes narrowed to slits. Juliet's heart lurched as it became clear that in another second, steam was going to start pouring out of his ears.

Uh-oh.

She took a step back, wondering if it was too late to retreat. Or flat-out run. She hoped the lock on her bedroom door was a strong one.

Not that she'd get the chance to find out. Before she could put even more distance between them, he reached out and snatched her wrist. His grip was firm, immovable, yet he wasn't hurting her, and she knew somehow that he wouldn't. That if she said anything, asked him to let go, he would do it.

He might not *let her go* let her go—as in let her walk away from the conversation he so clearly intended for them to have—but he wouldn't restrain her physically against her will.

Because of that, because she was nervous and uncomfortable, but not truly afraid of him, she didn't try to pull away. He was going to have questions, she understood that, and he deserved answers. Even if it meant meeting his show of temper head-on.

Rather than pulling her back out onto the porch, though, he turned her around and nudged her farther into the house.

"Pack your bags," he told her. "We're leaving."

"What? Wait. Why?" Tugging out of his hold, she twisted to face him.

"We're going back to New York. You're going to get checked out by a doctor, and then…"

He let the sentence trail off, she suspected because he didn't *know* what would come next and probably didn't want to make threats—or promises—he wasn't sure he'd be willing to carry out.

"No," she said with a shake of her head. "I told you, I'm not ready to go back there. Paul, my family… They'll ask questions, want answers I'm not prepared to give just yet. I came here to think, to *be alone* until I can get a better handle on things, and I still need to do that. I need some time to myself."

"Too bad," he replied, zero sympathy in his voice. "You don't get that luxury, not anymore. And neither do I."

A beat later, his tone softened. "Look, I just want to be sure. You were awfully sick this morning, too, so I'd like to know everything's okay. We'll stay at my place. No one else needs to know you're in the city until you're ready to see them. But we can't just stay here, doing nothing, pretending the problem doesn't exist as long as we don't go back to the real world."

Juliet tipped her head to one side, annoyed by his reference to her pregnancy as a "problem." She could hardly call him on it, though, since until very recently she'd thought of it exactly the same way. Even worse, she'd considered it something of a major catastrophe.

"What if you go back to the real world and leave me here to pretend awhile longer," she suggested hopefully.

His plan made sense, and she could understand his desire to be medically certain about what she was telling him, but she just wasn't mentally prepared to return to New York so soon. She'd barely gotten any time alone to sort things out, thanks to his unexpected arrival.

"Nice try," he replied with what could only be described as a smirk, "but not on your life. Now go pack your things and meet me back here in ten minutes or I'll toss you over my shoulder and carry you to the car, with or without your belongings."

She narrowed her eyes, her need to stand her ground warring with the fact that she believed Reid would do exactly what he said.

"Fine," she finally acquiesced.

She wasn't happy about it, but as long as he kept his word about letting her hide out at his brownstone, she supposed it wouldn't hurt to see a doctor and have the pregnancy confirmed. She should probably be on pre-natal vitamins and the like by now, anyway.

The only problem with staying with Reid was that they would be alone together for heaven knew how long. And wasn't that how she'd gotten herself into this mess in the first place?

They left Juliet's car at the lake house and drove back to the city in the Range Rover Reid had borrowed from his company's vehicle pool. She wasn't exactly happy about it, but he hadn't given her a choice. And he'd promised to make arrangements for a couple of his employees to drive to Vermont and bring the BMW back to New York for her. Of course, that would also require hiding it somewhere until she was ready to let her family know she'd returned—possibly in his corporate lot.

"Oh, what a tangled web we weave" kept dancing through his head as he drove, the only thing to fill the otherwise tense silence. He didn't like secrets, and he didn't like lies. It was part of the reason he'd become an investigator—to ferret out those sorts of details and set things right for the people who had been taken advantage of or betrayed.

Yet everything to do with the person sitting next to him seemed to be smothered in secrets and wrapped in lies. From the moment he'd met her. Worse, he'd found himself twisted up in his own share of both when he'd always prided himself on his solid and unwavering strength of character.

And he'd ignored the signs, made excuses, all because of the irresistible hold she apparently had over him.

And now there was a baby.

Maybe a baby. Not that he doubted Juliet's word, not about this, but mistakes could be made, and he would feel better hearing it from a medical professional after the proper tests had been conducted. Then and only then would he let himself start making any kind of plans for the future.

Reid's hands tightened on the steering wheel, his knuckles going white. He was pretty sure the entire thing was going to snap in two if he didn't loosen his grip soon. Behind his eyes, a headache was brewing.

How ironic that this would happen to him twice in a lifetime.

When he'd first met Valerie, he was in the army. Special Forces, to be precise. They'd been hot and heavy in the way only two young people with too many hormones running rampant and not enough common sense to keep them in check can.

Then she'd turned up pregnant. Valerie hadn't been the least bit happy about it, but surprisingly, Reid had. He'd been ready to settle down, ready to find something that would ground him and help him find a balance between what he did for a living and a normal, everyday life.

He hadn't been in love with Valerie as much as in lust, but with a kid on the way, he was more than prepared to marry her and do the whole modern-American-family thing.

The problem was, Valerie had no interest in marrying him or settling down to start that family. Instead, he found a note taped to his door not long after she'd told him about the baby, and she and the kid were both gone with the wind.

He'd thought about going after them, of course. Every day for a really long time, as a matter of fact. But if Valerie didn't want to be with him, didn't want him to be a father to her—their—child, then maybe it had been smarter of her to leave without telling him where she was going. For all he knew, she'd had an abortion on her way out of town, and the whole fatherhood thing was a moot point.

So he'd let them—her?—go. And maybe he'd started drinking a bit too much from time to time, but then, who could blame him?

Soon after that, he'd left the military and gone to work in private security, then private and corporate investigation, and finally opened his own firm. Once he was well and truly established with his first million in the bank and his first mention in *Forbes,* he'd actually put his skills to work and tracked them down after all.

Them. Valerie and his ten-year-old son, Theo.

She'd returned to West Texas to live with her family until the baby was born, and a few years after that married a lawyer from Dallas.

As far as Reid could tell, they were happy, and his son was being treated well. Whether or not Theo knew the attorney wasn't his real father, Reid wasn't sure. And unless there was a good reason to move in and shake up the boy's life, Reid had no intention of telling him.

But that didn't mean Reid didn't think about him. He wondered if his son liked science or sports, was into dinosaurs or train sets. And what his life would have been like if Valerie had stuck around and put up a white picket fence with him instead of running off to do as much with another man.

Not that it mattered, except for the fact that he now found himself in almost an identical situation with Juliet.

Reid's chest tightened as his thoughts and emotions from the past mixed and mingled with the present until he had trouble drawing a breath.

This time around, however, there was another man *already* in Juliet's life. Another man who could, conceivably, be the father of her unborn child.

Although, to be perfectly honest, Reid didn't think so. He believed Juliet when she said the baby was his. Otherwise she would have gone through with her wedding to the obnoxious jerk.

Why make her life more complicated for herself than it already was when she could have kept her mouth shut and simplified things exponentially? The first word he would have heard about Juliet having a child was if the birth announcement ended up in the paper.

So that was one problem that needed to be dealt with. Damned if he'd have Paul Harris butting in or causing trouble down the road. If Juliet truly was pregnant and the baby was his, then the ex-fiancé would have to go. On his own or with a bit of persuasion, Reid didn't particularly care which.

The next order of business would be what to *do* about the pregnancy.

Initially, the decision would be Juliet's, he knew that. No matter how he felt or what option she chose, he would have to take a step back for that one and let her do whatever she was going to do.

If she decided to keep it, though, he would have to make a few decisions of his own. Like whether to suggest they stay together and try to give the child a stable, two-parent home. Or go the separate homes/single parent/shared custody route.

One thing was for certain. He wasn't going to walk away this time. He wasn't going to let another woman give birth to his child without letting him be part of that child's life.

This time he would be involved.

This time he would be a real father, no matter what it took.

Juliet stared at her reflection in the mirror above the vanity of Reid's upstairs bathroom. It was a nice-size room: not too big and not too small, with cream-colored walls, oak trim and dark green ivy accents.

She wasn't surprised at the stylish décor that was neither too masculine nor too feminine. It matched the rest of the town house, which had also been professionally restored, furnished and decorated.

Thanks to a bit of makeup and the passing of her latest bout of morning sickness, she actually looked fresh and presentable. It was to Reid's credit that he'd made today's appointment with the doctor of his choice for early afternoon, *after* he knew any trouble she had with nausea would have passed.

He'd also put her in a room at the opposite end of the hall from his and stocked the downstairs refrigerator with clear soda and the cupboards with crackers, cream of wheat and soups he thought would be bland enough for her sensitive stomach.

As hosts went, he was being a kind and extremely accommodating one.

Why, then, was she such a knot of twisted, writhing nerve endings?

She'd been on pins and needles ever since he ordered her to collect her belongings and get in the car so he could drive her back to New York. But being under the same roof with him with so much tension simmering between them made her feel like a goldfish in a very small bowl. Staying in her room most of the time was akin to hiding inside her tiny plastic castle.

Now, though, she was dressed and ready not only to brave the outside world but to accompany Reid downtown to an unfamiliar doctor's office, where she would presumably be poked and prodded until tests either confirmed or denied that she was, indeed, pregnant.

Since she couldn't go back to the loft and risk being seen by Lily or Zoe or both, Juliet was living in the few items of warmer clothing she'd taken with her to the lake. Which meant that instead of a nice dress or skirt and heels like she would normally wear for an appointment of this type, she was wearing khaki slacks, a cream-colored knit sweater and a pair of comfortable—but dressy, thank goodness—ankle boots.

Glancing at the watch on her left wrist, she realized she couldn't spend any more time hiding out in the bathroom and took a deep, stabilizing breath as she pulled open the door.

Negotiating the long hallway and wide set of carpeted steps leading downstairs, she found Reid waiting for her near the front door. Waiting, if not patiently.

In slow, measured steps, he paced a few feet across the tiled foyer, stopped, checked his big, platinum watch face much as she had her own smaller one only moments before then turned on his heel and paced the same short length to where he'd begun. She caught him doing that twice as she descended the stairs.

As she reached the bottom, he stopped and turned in her direction, hands on hips.

"Ready?" he asked simply, but somewhat sharply.

Since she understood his impatience and anxiety, she didn't take it personally.

"Yes," she answered.

He removed her lightweight jacket from a row of hooks along the wall beside the door and helped her into it. To be perfectly honest, the spring temperatures in New York were probably too warm for both a sweater and jacket, but they'd agreed that she should look as nondescript as possible whenever she went out, for fear of being recognized. And she could always shed the jacket once she reached the car or doctor's office.

When she looked up from fastening the row of buttons at the front of the navy jacket and tying the belt at her waist, she found him holding a pair of dark-lensed, large-rimmed Jackie O sunglasses and a floppy, wide-brimmed hat.

"Better safe than sorry," he murmured, holding them out to her.

Though they made her feel somewhat awkward—possibly because they weren't her usual style and the hat didn't go with her coat *or* her handbag—she put them on and passed through the front door as he held it open for her. Going this incognito probably wasn't entirely necessary, but neither of them wanted to take the chance that she might run into someone she knew. Especially if, God forbid, Lily or Zoe were out and about today.

He led her to his Mercedes and helped her inside before moving around to the driver's side and sliding behind the wheel.

They rode in silence for several long minutes. Juliet found herself tapping and twisting her fingers, then realized she was fidgeting and forced herself to stop.

There was nothing to be nervous about, she told herself. Only finding out definitively that she was pregnant and then having to deal with whatever fallout of that knowledge came from the father of her child.

Nope, not a thing to be nervous about.

"Are you cool enough under all those layers? I can turn the air on, if you like."

At the sound of his voice filling the previously catacomb-quiet interior, Juliet jumped. Even though his tone was much softer than before, she swallowed, laying her palms flat on her upper thighs. "No, thank you, I'm fine."

Another beat passed and then he asked, "How are you feeling? Better?"

With a small smile, she nodded, glancing at him from the corner of her eye. "The soda and crackers help."

She started to say thank-you again but was afraid of sounding like a broken record. Besides, she didn't want him thinking she was *too* grateful. He'd forced her to come back to New York with him after all. And once they confirmed that she truly was pregnant, she wouldn't allow him to run roughshod over her and make her feel beholden.

The rest of the trip, made longer than necessary by typical bumper-to-bumper Manhattan traffic, passed without further conversation. When they arrived at the building that held the doctor's suite of offices, Reid parked in the underground garage, then escorted her into the elevator and up to the twenty-seventh floor.

While he checked them in at the reception desk, she found an empty spot in the waiting area and took a seat. A few minutes later, a nurse called her back to fill out some initial paperwork.

She could have handled the simple question-and-answer session just fine on her own, but Reid insisted on accompanying her. If the nurse thought his behavior odd—or found it intimidating that he leaned against the wall, towering over them with his arms folded across his impressive chest—she didn't let it show.

Juliet answered questions, had her blood pressure, pulse and temperature taken, and even allowed the nurse to take a vial of blood before being shown to a private examination room, where she was instructed to strip. To her surprise, Reid offered to stay outside while she undressed, but asked her to give a shout when she was once again covered by the thin gown the nurse had provided so he could return.

Despite Reid's money and influence—two things she was sure he'd used in order to secure an appointment with an exclusive gynecologist in such a short amount of time—they still ended up waiting in the examination room for long, interminable minutes until the doctor arrived.

She sat on the end of the examination table, feeling a bit like a deli sandwich as paper crinkled beneath her, while Reid took the single chair situated along the opposite wall. The clock behind her ticked off the seconds until Juliet thought she might scream.

Finally, there was a knock at the door and the doctor entered, greeting both her and Reid with a firm hand-shake. A manila folder containing her test results in hand, he lowered himself onto the low, wheeled stool at the end of the exam table and smiled warmly.

Splitting his attention equally between his new patient and the man who would be paying the bill, he said, "I know you're eager to have the big question answered, so why don't we get right to it. Congratulations—you are, in fact, expecting."

Juliet hadn't noticed how tight her chest was until she released her breath on a whoosh. And Reid must have been equally tense, because she heard his exhalation from across the room.

His face, however, was a blank slate. She couldn't tell whether he was happy or disappointed, upset or indifferent. Which only caused her chest to grow tight again. The doctor's continued friendliness helped to put her at ease, though.

"How would you feel about an ultrasound? We can get a look at your little peanut and maybe get an idea of how far along you are."

The thought of seeing the baby, even as tiny as it must be and on the fuzzy black-and-white screen of an ultrasound machine, brought a lump to her throat.

Swallowing hard and blinking back the moisture that stung her eyes, she nodded eagerly. "Yes, please."

She spared a glance for Reid, who stood up and moved to the head of the examination table with her while the doctor got everything ready. She almost reached for his hand, part of her wishing he would reach for her.

But then, they weren't a normal expectant couple, were they? They were just two people who had happened to make a baby together.

Nine

Reid sat in his darkened study, a glass of scotch on the desk in front of him, the open bottle right next to it. He threw back the two fingers of amber liquid, then poured himself another, his gaze never leaving the printed picture in his hand.

If he didn't know what he was looking at, he would have thought it was some peculiar three-dimensional puzzle picture of the Loch Ness Monster or a crater on the moon.

But he did know what he was looking at. The peanut, as the doctor had called it. His son or daughter.

It was too soon to tell which, but even if it hadn't been, Juliet had begged the doctor not to reveal the baby's gender. She wanted it to be a surprise, and Reid was fine with that. He'd had more than enough surprises for one week, thank you very much.

He was going to be a father. Again. And once again it was with a woman who didn't necessarily intend to let him be part of his child's life.

He'd never thought his relationship with Valerie was complicated, and look how that had turned out.

On the other hand, Juliet was complicated with a capital *C*. He'd known that the minute she'd walked into his office at McCormack Investigations asking him to find her sister.

Now, on top of everything else, she was pregnant. He wasn't sure there was a word in the dictionary for how complicated that made this.

Taking another belt of scotch, he slid open the center drawer of the desk and laid the sonogram picture safely inside. Then, pushing to his feet, he left the study and slowly climbed the stairs to the second floor.

Juliet's bedroom door was closed, just as it had been since soon after they arrived home.

After the appointment, he'd driven back to the brownstone without a word being spoken between them. She'd fixed herself a bite to eat for lunch and offered to make him something, too, but he'd declined. He definitely hadn't been in the mood for food.

He hadn't been in the mood to talk, either, though she'd asked if he wanted to. He gave her credit for that: for being willing to open up and discuss their situation rather than zipping her lips and cutting him out of anything related to the pregnancy.

He just hoped she was still feeling chatty, because now he *was* ready to talk. And he intended to make her listen.

Juliet was sitting cross-legged on her bed, sketch pad on her lap. She'd begun with the intention of doing a bit more work on the new handbag sketches she'd started up at the lake house, but instead all of her doodles seemed to turn into baby bonnets and booties.

With a huff, she scribbled over her latest version of the bassinet she could already picture in the corner of her room back at the loft. As supportive as she knew her sisters would be about having a little niece or nephew to spoil rotten, she was pretty sure they wouldn't be gung ho about adding a line of infant wear to Zaccaro Fashions.

Besides, there were a few more important issues to deal with before she started shopping for furniture for a nursery or suggesting a new design direction to Lily and Zoe.

A knock sounded at the door, and her heart plummeted to her stomach. There was one of the important issues now.

Turning her sketch pad over and setting it aside, Juliet straightened her legs and crossed them at the ankle before calling out, "Come in."

Reid entered, the top few buttons of his white dress shirt undone, the soft cotton material a lot less crisp than it had been a few hours earlier. She pretended not to notice the V of tanned skin visible at his throat or his strong forearms with his cuffs rolled to his elbows.

He left the door open, which wasn't necessary, but did make her feel moderately more comfortable. Less like a small woodland animal cornered by a dangerous predator.

The good news was that he looked much less angry himself, less trapped than he had when they'd left for the doctor's office. On the way back, he'd just looked vacant, on the verge of stunned.

Totally understandable. Which was why she'd brought her lunch upstairs and given him some time alone. To think, or come to terms, or whatever else he needed to do after learning that their little safe sex fling hadn't been quite so safe after all.

He stood staring at her, hands in his pockets. He didn't seem to know what to say, though she was certain there was something on his mind or he wouldn't have knocked to begin with.

"Reid," she said at the exact same time he said, "Juliet."

Blowing out a breath, he inclined his head. "You first."

She wasn't entirely sure what to say herself, but knew they had to start somewhere. Swinging her legs over the side of the bed, she sat up straighter.

"I know you believe me now," she told him. "About the baby. And I know you believe it's yours. I wouldn't even say it if I weren't sure it was true. I hadn't been with Paul that way for quite a while before we... You know. And not after, either," she clarified.

She waited, watching his eyes, praying she wouldn't see doubt or distrust there. Relief washed over her when his gaze not only remained steadfast, but he offered her a nod of agreement, as well.

"But I don't want you to think I expect anything of you," she continued. "You can be as involved as you're comfortable with. I'm not after your money, either. I mean, I know you and your company are worth quite a bit, and I know that probably makes you suspicious of women you think might be gold diggers. But I'm financially independent myself, and my family is well-off enough on top of that to help me if I need anything.

So you don't have to worry that I'll come after you for support or try to—" she lifted one shoulder carelessly "—shake you down or anything like that."

One dark brow rose on the "shake you down" part, which she had felt sort of silly even saying out loud.

"Are you finished?" he asked in a low voice.

Not exactly the response she'd expected, but okay. "Yes."

"I have one question."

She swallowed hard. "All right."

"Are you going to keep it?"

For a second, her heart stopped and her throat closed up, making her think that her morning sickness might not be sticking to just mornings anymore. Without conscious thought, her hand moved to cover her abdomen protectively.

"Of course," she replied sharply. She shouldn't have been offended by the question, but she was, and her tone reflected as much.

Long minutes passed in silence while their gazes locked, but neither of them moved. Then Reid pulled his hands from his pockets, lifting one to rub at his slightly stubbled jaw. After a moment, he let his arm drop and gave a brusque, decisive jerk of his head.

"In that case," he said, "I think we should get married."

Juliet blinked. There were a lot of things she'd thought he might say, a lot of conversations she'd expected to have over the next few months with the father of her unborn child. But of all the topics she'd imagined, that definitely had *not* been one of them.

"Excuse me?"

His jaw popped as he took a deep breath, not looking at all pleased that he had to repeat himself. "I think we should get married," he said again.

The words had a razor-sharp edge to them the second time around, and the first hadn't exactly been Peter Cottontail soft to begin with.

As kindly as she could, Juliet shook her head and said, "No."

Reid's eyes narrowed, pupils going round as BBs within his toffee-brown irises. "No?"

His voice held a hint of bitterness, warning even, that she had to ignore. *Made* herself ignore, despite the shiver that skated down her spine.

Juliet was surprised by just how much it had hurt to utter that single word, but she'd done it all the same. Then she licked her lips, put her shoulders back and said it again. "I'm sorry, but no."

Placing her palms flat on either side of her hips, she let her gaze fall to the carpeted floor for a moment as she shook her head.

"I know what you're trying to do. And I appreciate it, I really do," she said softly. "But it's not necessary. You don't have to make the grand gesture or make an honest woman of me. I'll be fine. The baby and I will both be fine, and you'll have full access, just as I promised. I won't cut you off simply because I don't have a ring on my finger."

She rubbed the underside of the bare digit where Paul's engagement ring had rested until only a few days ago. Now Reid was trying to stick another one on there, and she wasn't sure she was ready for that. Not under these circumstances.

"That's not what I'm doing," he objected through clenched teeth.

Her mouth curved in a gentle smile as she lifted her face back to his. "Yes, it is. But I just ran away from one wedding, I'm not in a big rush to race toward another."

His nostrils flared as he glared at her with the same dark, stormy expression she was sure he used to intimidate bad guys and get information from reluctant witnesses. It was a good glare, but she held her ground.

"Do you think I wouldn't be a good father?" he practically snapped. "Or a good husband? Is that it?"

She leaned back, stunned by the outburst. "Of course not."

She honestly hadn't given it much thought. As far as Reid's potential as a parent was concerned, she hadn't been pregnant long enough to reflect upon every little detail of child rearing that might come along. And she'd never seen marriage to Reid as any part of her future—with or without a child between them.

But now that he'd brought it up, she took a moment to give it a good, hard sixty-second dissection.

She could only imagine that Reid would be an exceptional father. He was strong, brave, self-assured, successful and—at least in her experience—selfless.

He would put his child's interests and needs above all else, always. He would be protective but understanding. Strict but also kind and loving. And she hoped fun.

There had been an underlying level of tension to their relationship from the beginning, but they'd had fun, too. She knew he had a sense of humor and suspected that he would be happy to take his child to the park, or kick off his shoes and play along in the sandbox. Which was important in a child's life and, she realized, important to her.

So yes, she thought he would be a good father.

And when he found a woman he truly loved, she had no doubt he would make an excellent husband. All of the same qualities that made him good father material—protectiveness, successfulness, selflessness—would make him an exceptional partner, as well.

She could more than easily picture coming home to him each evening…or perhaps having him come home to her instead. Doing the whole "hi, honey, how was your day?" routine. Eating dinner together, putting the kids to bed. And then later, taking their time putting themselves to bed. She knew all too well how satisfying *that* part of a marriage to Reid McCormack would be.

Shaking herself free of her reflections and the memories that had her core temperature rising a few errant degrees, she amended that last thought. It would be satisfying *for some other woman*. Not for her. Because marriage to Reid wasn't in the cards for her.

Oh, he'd asked, but she'd turned him down for more than simply the reasons she'd stated.

It was true that she didn't want to rush into another "here comes the bride" situation so soon after making such a fiasco of the first one.

And she most certainly didn't want to get married only because she was pregnant. Marriage was hardly the best resolution for Reid's guilt trip.

But the real reason she'd rejected his proposal—as off the cuff and questionably sincere as it had been—was that she never again wanted to be engaged to, almost married to, or even seriously involved with someone who didn't love her madly.

She'd gone that route once, doing what was expected more than following her own heart, and look how that had turned out.

So, no. The next time she said yes and agreed to wear a man's ring on her finger for the rest of her life, it would be because she was head over heels in love with him, and he with her. End of story.

Meeting his eyes and making sure he knew she meant what she was about to tell him, she said, "I think you'll be a wonderful father. And an equally good husband someday."

He canted his head to one side, studying her. "Someday. But not today, and not with you, hmm?"

The sad smile she offered was as wide as she could make it. "No."

Catching her off guard, he stepped forward, stopping only when their knees brushed. She glanced down to where the black of his slacks met the light tan of hers and then back up to his face.

He grasped her elbows and hauled her up until her breasts were pressed to his chest, the air knocked from her lungs by astonishment alone.

"Are you afraid we won't be compatible?" he asked, his voice low and thick, falling like dark, aged rum on all of her most sensitive places. "In the long-term?"

She opened her mouth to reply, but her tongue felt like a giant wad of cotton, making it impossible to speak. Nearly impossible to breathe.

Compatibility was seriously not an issue. At least not the kind of compatibility he was currently talking about.

Running his hand along her jaw and around the back of her neck, he threaded his fingers into the hair at her nape and tipped her head back, following with his mouth. He didn't give her time to think or to stop him— not that she would have tried.

His lips, warm and soft and tasting of what she

thought might have been scotch, simply covered hers. She would rather taste the rich liquor on his tongue than from a glass any day of the week.

Juliet wasn't sure if he truly desired her, or if he was just trying to prove a point, but she couldn't seem to find it in herself to push him away. There was so much between them. So many complicated issues, so much said and unsaid. The last thing either of them needed was to add another intimate encounter to the list.

But as he kissed her, as his mouth moved against hers, his tongue licking and tickling and teasing, she didn't care. Or at the very least, she was willing to push everything else to a back burner to be dealt with later. Much later.

Her hands moved up to cup his shoulders, his tight muscles flexing beneath the fine cotton weave of his shirt. He was exactly as she remembered him—strong and warm and overtly masculine.

Without breaking the kiss, Reid backed her the short distance to the bed. When she bumped the edge of the mattress and started to fall, he fell with her, sinking onto the soft surface, covering her with his weight and power and sexual intent.

It reminded her so much of their first time. The passion, the need, the intensity. The way he took control and possessed her without ever making her feel constrained or dominated.

While her arms lowered to caress the expanse of his back, his hands drifted down to her waist and slipped under the hem of her knit top. The pads of his fingers danced across her bare skin, pushing the sweater upward. Higher and higher, taking away her ability to draw oxygen into her lungs.

Hoping to repay the erotic favor, she trailed her hands around to his front, deftly loosening his belt, unfastening his slacks and slipping her fingers inside. Reid groaned into her mouth, and she swallowed the sound even as she reveled in it, let it empower her. She pushed the trousers down over his hips at the same time she lifted her arms to allow him to tug the sweater all the way off over her head.

They were both breathing heavily as she floated back to the mattress. Their gazes locked, and she could see herself reflected in the sable brown of his eyes, along with raw heat and longing.

He began to trail nibbling kisses everywhere he could reach—her mouth, her chin, the corners of her eyes, back down the column of her throat to the valley between her breasts. He cupped them together with her bra still in place, teasing the budding nipples with his thumbs through the material.

Juliet released a sigh, letting the sensations roll through her, letting them fill her and build and spill over. She ran her hands down the center of his chest, releasing the tiny buttons of his dress shirt as she went until she could slip her fingers inside and push the material apart.

He had to let go of her breasts and shift to allow her to remove the shirt altogether, but it was no great loss since it gave her the chance to stroke his firm, sun-bronzed skin. The smooth flesh that covered rock-hard muscles and tendons, that flexed and flowed beneath her touch.

She pushed the shirt over his shoulders and down his arms, letting it fall to the floor behind him. Her hands found the upper curve of his buttocks and she

gave them a gentle squeeze before running her nails up
the line of his spine.

A shudder vibrated down the length of his back, air
hissing through his teeth on an exhale. Juliet grinned
at the untamed response, but her amusement was short-
lived when he growled low in his throat and grasped her
ankles, shoving her farther onto the bed. She clutched at
the covers to keep from falling as he yanked her boots
off one at a time, then reached for the waist of her pants
and peeled them down her legs in a single swift motion
before the second boot hit the floor.

His actions left her in nothing but her bra and underwear, and he quickly toed off his own shoes, kicked
out of his trousers and stepped between her parted legs.
He ran the flat of one palm up the center of her body,
from the lacy band of her French-cut panties, over the
still-flat plane of her abdomen, to her rib cage and between her breasts. Then he caught her under the arms
and hauled her into a sitting position.

He stared deep into her eyes, his hot breath spilling
across her face as she pressed against him once again.
She hitched her legs high over his hips, keeping him
close while his arms snaked around to the rear clasp
of her bra. With a flick of his thumb and forefingers,
the elastic gave way, the straps and modest cups falling
away from her body.

She helped him free her arms from the garment, then
arched off the bed as he went for her underwear. He disposed of his own at the same time but didn't give her a
chance to admire his arousal before hauling her up and
turning around to take her place on the edge of the bed.

He brought her down on top of him, so she was strad-
dling his lap. The heat of his erection pressed between

them, but he didn't move to use it. Instead, he splayed his hands at her sides and brought her in to capture her mouth. While his tongue slipped past her lips to tease and taunt, he caressed her back, up to her shoulder blades, back down to her waist and the globes of her bottom.

With his hands on her buttocks, she lifted up, moaning as her swollen, sensitized breasts rubbed against his chest. The kiss deepened as they shifted, moved exactly as they needed to until he was poised at her opening, brushing but not quite ready to enter.

She clawed at his biceps, the muscles bulging beneath her fingertips as he clutched at her hips in return. But no matter how many times she canted her pelvis or tried to lower herself onto his length, he held her just out of reach.

"Reid," she groaned in frustration.

When she opened her eyes, he was smiling up at her much as she imagined a wolf would smile over a stag once it had run it to ground and was getting ready to devour—gleaming teeth and all.

"Let's see just how compatible we are," he murmured in a voice so low she almost didn't hear him.

And then he pulled her down, sliding inside of her in one long, powerful glide.

Juliet sucked in a breath, letting her head fall back and her lashes flutter closed as she acclimated herself to his size, his heat, his possession. Beneath her, Reid remained equally still. She could hear the air sawing in and out of his lungs, but otherwise it was almost as though he was afraid to move.

She was pretty sure she knew precisely how he felt. Not only because being with him like this put her on the teetering precipice of losing control, but it felt like forever since they'd been together.

It wasn't just the sex, it was the nearness, the intimacy. When they were together, like this, without quarrels and conflicts between them, things were amazing. They connected in a way she never had with any other man.

Unfortunately, there *were* quarrels and conflicts between them. Almost too many to count. And as much as she might have enjoyed it otherwise, they couldn't stay naked and in bed 24/7. If only.

But for now, they *were* naked and in bed. For now, the gulf of problems between them was forgotten and there was only the physical, a whirlpool of sensation dragging them both down.

Reid's mouth found the underside of her jaw, his lips and teeth and slight beard stubble scraping her there. She pushed up on her knees, drawing away from him, and they both gasped. Then, with the help of his hands glued to either side of her hips, she moved back down.

A hiss accompanied her descent, though whether the sound came from him or from her, she couldn't be sure. And then it didn't matter. The room filled with sighs and moans and heavy breathing, along with every manner of other inarticulate noises as she rose and fell, as he plunged inside of her again and again.

If it hadn't been for his hold on her—strong almost to the point of pain and completely assured—she was pretty sure she would have fallen several times over. Right off the edge of the bed and flat on her butt...or worse.

But Reid didn't let her fall. He barely budged himself, even as their activities became nearly acrobatic.

As tension mounted, pleasure building at her core, she tightened her hold on the only anchor in her rapidly spiraling universe. Her hands curled into the meat of his shoulders like talons, her legs circling his waist in a viselike grip.

"Reid." She panted his name over and over, unsure whether the sound was actually passing her lips or was merely an ongoing chant inside her head.

He whispered her name in return, and that was all it took to send her flying. Her entire body went rigid, her spine bowing as a single tremendous orgasm tore through her, followed by a series of small but no less intense ones.

Shimmers of pleasure continued to rock her as Reid's fingers dug into the flesh of her hips and buttocks, and he gave one final pump upward before shouting his completion into the curve of her neck.

Her face was buried against his throat while she struggled for breath and Reid's chest rose and fell choppily against her. Another second of almost suspended animation passed before the strength seemed to go out of his muscles and he fell backward, taking Juliet with him.

Long minutes later, after their breathing had returned to normal and she was telling herself to get up even as sleep pulled at her, Reid's voice reached up to stir the hair near her ear.

"I'd say that we passed."

Rolling her head to rest on the upper portion of his chest to face him a bit more fully, she made an indistinct sound low in her throat. "Passed what?"

A chuckle rumbled beneath her. "The compatibility test."

"Mmm."

Since that had never been a question in her mind, she didn't want to say too much one way or the other. Especially when she knew this had all been his way of proving a point...and convincing her that "compatibility" should translate into "commitment."

Something she would be only too eager to agree to if circumstances were different. But she couldn't let a surprise pregnancy and his sense of chivalry push her into a situation she didn't think either of them were ready for.

"But you're not going to change your mind, are you?" he asked quietly. "About marrying me."

Holding her breath and hoping her answer didn't completely destroy the nice little bubble of contentment surrounding her, she said, "Not today."

After another stretch of tense silence, he sighed but didn't let go of her and didn't sit up and walk out. Instead, he stayed exactly where he was, with his arm growing even tighter around her waist.

Ten

When Juliet next awoke, she was alone in her bed. Or the bed in the guest room of Reid's town house, at any rate.

Though Reid was no longer lying naked beneath her, acting as the best human mattress ever, he had apparently shifted her around so that her head was on one of the pillows near the headboard and she was covered up to her chin by the sheets and lightweight comforter.

Throwing back the covers and pushing to the edge of the bed, she blew out a breath. She didn't know whether to categorize this most recent encounter as a failure or a success. A little of each, she supposed.

But for now, at least, Reid seemed willing to let the topic of a shotgun wedding drop.

She had no doubt Reid McCormack was in her life to stay—which was only right, since they would soon share a child. But while she couldn't agree to marry him—because he'd suggested it for all the wrong reasons—that didn't mean she wasn't still attracted to him. Sort of overwhelmingly, distractedly attracted, if she was completely honest.

Even now, the scent of his cologne reached out from the tangled bedclothes and made her want to breathe deep. The same as it had the entire time they were involved. The same as it did every time they were in the same room together, to the point where she was perpetually tempted to crook a finger and invite him to take her to bed.

A flush of heat warmed her from her hairline straight down to the tips of her wine-colored toenails. Flashes of her collective time with him filled her head. All the meals they'd shared, the conversations they'd had. All of the other times she'd been in this house with him, often wandering around nude under Reid's oversize robe after they'd already made love or whiling away the hours in bed with him. His big, king-size bed, not this one.

She wished they could go back there, when things were—ironically—simpler.

Which made her realize that she really needed to leave. She couldn't stay here, wishing they could go back in time or that things could be different when they were never going to be.

And having Reid propose to her—as rough around the edges as that proposal had been—only aided in driving home the fact that she was hiding. Hiding from Paul, hiding from her family, hiding from reality.

But she couldn't hide forever, and the longer she did, the weaker she would appear. The harder it would be to return to her old life.

She was also afraid that if she let Reid host and protect her any longer, especially with side benefits like the ones they'd recently shared, he would continue to see her as *needing* his help and protection. But she didn't want to be a job for him, a responsibility. Not like this.

It was time to get back on her feet and set herself up as the strong, independent mother she would need to be when this baby arrived.

Decision made, she hopped off the bed, reached for her discarded clothes and started to pack.

Packed and ready to go, Juliet made her way downstairs. Reid wasn't on the second floor, so she knew he had to be down here someplace, she just wasn't sure where or whether or not he'd want to see her.

He might not be in the mood to deal with her again so soon. Maybe he regretted what they'd done or was still upset that she'd turned down his knee-jerk proposal.

But she wouldn't feel right sneaking out and leaving only a note, so she left her bag by the front door and went searching for him. She found him in his study, the lights off, a fire roaring in the fireplace, and a bottle of liquor on his desk that looked as though he'd been nursing it for several hours.

A pang of guilt went through her at the sight. Had she done that to him? Driven him to empty an entire bottle of…whatever strong alcohol it was with her secrets and dropped bombs and refusal to let him step up and save the day?

But she didn't want him to rescue her, not out of obligation.

Steeling herself for the confrontation that she suspected was about to happen, she tapped on the door-jamb to get his attention.

His head snapped up and he turned away from his computer screen to face her. She caught a glimpse of his knit brow and the lines of displeasure bracketing his mouth before he realized he was scowling and cleared his features.

"I'm sorry to bother you," she said, taking a single step into the room, "but I wanted to let you know that I'm leaving."

"Leaving?" The knit brow and frown lines reappeared. "Why?"

"I'm going home. It's time. I can't hide out here forever, any more than I could have hidden up at the lake house forever. I need to face up to my mistakes, come clean with Paul and let my family know what's going on."

Her fingers found the knob of the open door and wrapped around the cool brass. "Thank you for everything. Back at the cabin and…here. You were more patient and understanding than I probably deserved, given the circumstances."

"You don't have to do that," he said gruffly, his own hands curled into fists on the flat surface of the desk before loosening again. "Leave or thank me."

She smiled softly. "Yes, I do. But I'll be in touch. And you know where to find me. I won't disappear again, I promise."

Juliet didn't know what kind of reaction she'd expected, but it wasn't the complete and utter silence that followed her final statement or the blank, verging on annoyed look on his face. When a couple more minutes

ticked by with no further response from him, she decided this must be his way of dismissing her.

The alternative was that he was too furious with her
to speak. Either way, she figured exiting stage left as
quickly as possible was probably her best option.

Inclining her head in one last goodbye, she slowly
backed out of the study and walked toward the front
of the house, where her bag and a car from the service
she'd called were waiting.

Not sure what kind of reception she would receive
when she arrived home, Juliet let herself into the loft
with her key. She wasn't sneaking, exactly, but she was
trying to be relatively quiet.

She needn't have bothered. Lily and Zoe were both
standing at the kitchen island. Zoe's back was to the
door as she leaned negligently against the countertop,
one knee resting on a stool and her sparkling, bejeweled
stiletto dangling from the tips of her toes. Lily, however,
was facing Juliet's direction, a large bowl in front of
her as she tossed what looked to be salad ingredients.

At the sound of the front door softly clicking closed,
both of her sisters' heads popped up and their eyes went
wide.

"Juliet!" Lily cried, dropping the utensils and coming around the island.

At the same time, Zoe uttered a typical "Oh, my God"
before stomping her foot back into her shoe and clicking
along behind Lily as they made a beeline for her.

For the next several heartbeats she was surrounded
and smothered and hugged within an inch of her life.
And despite the inability to breathe, Juliet cherished
the sensation, tears prickling behind her closed eyelids.

No matter what she ever did, how much trouble she might get herself into or how crazy she might act at times, she knew her sisters would always be there for her. They would accept her, support her and, just like now, welcome her with open arms.

There was a lot of sniffing and blinking and happy laughter from the three of them as they separated, but it didn't take long for her sisters' expressions to turn accusatory. Lily even put her hands on her hips.

"Where have you been?" she wanted to know. "We've been worried sick."

"Well, until Reid McCormack called to say he'd located you and that you were okay," Zoe supplied. "Then we were just plain worried, especially when he wouldn't tell us *where* you were or when you planned to come home."

"I know. I'm so sorry," Juliet said, reaching for their hands and giving them each a squeeze so they would know just how sincere her apology was.

"There's...a lot going on, and I promise to tell you everything now that I'm back. But I couldn't go through with the wedding and needed some time to myself to think about what I *was* going to do before I came home."

There was a heavy pause while Lily and Zoe considered that. And then Lily leaned in to give her another quick, hard hug.

"We're just glad you're all right. And we're ready to listen whenever you're ready to share. Whatever it is that sent you running..." Lily gave a low chuckle. "Well, I've been there, done that. You forgave me for keeping secrets, and I'm sure Zoe and I can forgive you for yours. Right, Zoe?"

Their youngest sister got an elbow to the ribs, which

she took like a drama queen—yowling in feigned pain, rubbing her side, hitting Lily back. But under it all, Juliet knew that Zoe was equally happy to have her back and every ounce as there for her as Lily was.

She made that clear when she grew serious and turned sky-blue eyes on her. "Girls in glass slippers shouldn't throw stones. As long as you and Lily keep putting up with me, I'll keep putting up with you."

Juliet gave her baby sister a watery smile before pulling her close. "Deal."

After a few more minutes of excessive hugging, Lily carried Juliet's things farther into the apartment and said, "We were just fixing dinner. Do you want to go upstairs and unpack or maybe take a nap before we eat?"

Juliet rolled her eyes in self-deprivation. "I'm pretty much napped out for the time being, believe me."

Lily and Zoe both gave her odd looks, but she waved them off. She would explain *everything* soon enough.

"Let me take my stuff to my room, and then I'll come back down and help. What are we having?"

"Pizza," the two of them singsonged at exactly the same time.

"Perfect," she said, and meant it.

The scent of baking crust filled the loft. There would be mile-high veggies in deference to Zoe's vegetarian preferences, and wine or soda or sometimes even beer while the three of them cozied up on the couch to watch a movie or talk about their weeks. In this case, she suspected she would be doing most of the talking while her sisters listened eagerly. And, boy, did she have a tale to tell!

While Zoe and Lily returned to the kitchen, Juliet carried her overnight bag upstairs and put a few items away. Makeup bag on the bathroom vanity; dirty laundry in the hamper. She changed out of her lake house clothes and into a more comfortable pair of yoga pants and a soft, roomy cotton tunic top, the better to lounge around in while she caught up with her sisters.

Heading back down to the main living area of the loft, she joined Zoe and Lily at the island, offering a hand wherever necessary. They made small talk the entire time, keeping things light. Juliet let Lily and Zoe fill her in on what *they'd* been up to since her failed wedding ceremony, saving her own long and winding tale until they were settled in with their meal and she could tell them everything they needed to know without interruption.

An hour later, all three of them were perched cross-legged on the sofa with small plates of salad, large plates of piping-hot pizza and glasses of fizzing cola on the coffee table in front of them.

It took five, maybe ten seconds from the time their butts hit the cushions for Lily to cock her head, pull a chunk of broccoli from the top of her slice and say, "Okay, spill," before popping the green floret into her mouth.

Taking a deep breath and realizing she was probably going to be doing a lot more talking than eating, Juliet started at the beginning and didn't stop until she was well and truly finished.

She told them about the first time she'd met with Reid at his office to discuss Lily's disappearance, when she'd run off to Los Angeles to find out who was stealing her designs.

She confessed her instant attraction to the too-handsome-for-*her*-own-good investigator, and the guilt she'd felt over thinking about him at all when she was already engaged to Paul.

From there, she knew it wouldn't be a terribly big leap for Lily and Zoe to see where the story was going. But she'd promised all, and so she told them. About Paul's slowly increasing abuse, Reid's discovery of bruises and his anger at her fiancé's treatment of her, of that first night they'd spent together and how she'd broken up with Paul immediately afterward only to carry on a clandestine, nearly forbidden affair with Reid for the next few months....

And she told them about the pressure she'd felt from Paul and their families to go through with the wedding after all.

Finally, she admitted her reason—reasons?—for running away on her wedding day. The stick turning blue, and her rather sudden realization that she couldn't walk down the aisle and say "I do" to Paul while carrying another man's child. Especially while she still had feelings—as confusing, mixed up and jumbled as they were—for that other man.

Juliet wasn't sure what her sisters'—especially Zoe's—record was for how many times they could utter "ohmigosh, ohmigosh, ohmigosh" in a row, but she was pretty sure they broke it. But even given their complete and total astonishment at her long list of admissions, when they finally stopped gaping like guppies, they zeroed in on *exactly* the right aspect of her narration.

"You're pregnant?" Zoe nearly squealed.

Lily's reaction didn't include the squeal, but only because her smile was already so wide and beaming. "Oh, Juliet, that's wonderful! Congratulations."

Almost simultaneously, they set aside their empty

plates and cocooned her again in delighted sisterly embraces.

When they pulled away, Lily tucked a loose strand of blond hair behind her ear and asked, "So have you told Reid about the baby?"

Juliet nodded and filled them in on the rest—Reid tracking her down at the lake house, catching her in the most embarrassing throes of morning sickness and how she had to tell him about the baby whether she was ready or not. Then coming back to New York and staying with him until the doctor of his choice confirmed the pregnancy.

"Oh, no," Zoe groaned, covering her face with one hand. "We never should have asked him to help us find you. We messed up everything."

"Of course you didn't," Juliet assured her, peeling her sister's fingers from her eyes and giving them a squeeze. "I would have told him eventually anyway. He has a right to know he's going to be a father after all. And it gave us a chance to work things out. For me to let him know I'm not going to ask him for anything, but won't try to keep him away from the baby, either."

Lily's brows dipped. "That's it? You told him you were pregnant and all he said was 'okay'?"

Juliet rolled a shoulder, pretending her sister's frank assessment of the situation didn't bother her. "Pretty much. I don't want him to feel trapped, and I'm not going to marry him just because I'm pregnant."

It was Zoe's turn to furrow her brow. "He asked you to marry him?"

Clearing her throat, Juliet avoided her sisters' too-sharp scrutiny and leaned forward to retrieve her glass of soda. Taking a small sip, she said, "Yes, but I turned him down. He only did it out of obligation, and I'm no-where near ready to try to make it down the aisle again for all the wrong reasons."

That little revelation was met with silence as her sisters exchanged looks, but neither of them challenged her or tried to change her mind. A moment later, Lily nodded and Zoe reached out to pat Juliet's knee.

"Whatever you need, however you want to handle this, we're here for you," Lily told her.

"And ohmigosh, we're going to be *aunts!*" Zoe practically shrieked, bouncing up and down on the sofa cushion.

There was another long stretch of laughter and talk of whether the baby would be a boy or a girl, nursery colors and themes and the like. Then, as they all filled their plates with a second slice of pizza, Juliet turned the conversation to serious matters once again.

"Did Mom and Dad go home after the wedding was called off?" she asked.

"They stuck around for a while," Lily answered, "until we heard from Reid that he'd located you and you were safe. They weren't thrilled when he wouldn't say where you were, but we told them we'd stay on top of things and keep them informed along the way. That was enough to convince them to go back to Connecticut, but they call every single day to see if we've heard anything new from or about you."

The icky, oily feeling of guilt slid through Juliet, and she lowered her gaze to the floor. "I need to go up there and see them. Apologize." Lifting her head, she sighed. "I should talk to Paul, too."

"You don't owe him anything," Zoe snapped, anger lighting her blue eyes.

Lily's own protective frown was nearly a mirror image of their younger sister's. "I agree. He deserves a good, swift kick to the you-know-what, not an apology."

"I can't argue with you there," Juliet murmured. "I should have broken things off with him so much sooner."

"The minute he laid a finger on you," Zoe grumbled.

"Absolutely," Juliet conceded, still wondering why she hadn't. "And stuck to the decision the first time I told him I didn't want to marry him instead of convincing myself to give him another chance. But leaving him at the altar was a lousy thing to do. I feel like I should at least see him face-to-face and tell him I'm sorry for any embarrassment I caused."

"Humph," Zoe huffed.

"If you're set on doing that," Lily said, "I think one of us should go with you."

"I'll do it!" Zoe declared with a bounce. "I've got nothing better to do, but somebody needs to stay here and take care of the store, and Nigel is flying in from Los Angeles soon, so I know you'll want to be here for that," she said to Lily.

Then she wiggled her brows and shot Lily a teasing grin. "Just think—you'll have the whole loft to yourselves."

"Well, that certainly would be nice," Lily replied with a smile and a faint hint of color rising to her cheeks.

Rolling her eyes in amusement, Zoe said, "Do me a favor, though—Lysol any public surfaces when you're done. I don't need to eat my corn flakes at the kitchen island knowing my soon-to-be brother-in-law's bare butt was on it first."

Eleven

If there was one thing Reid excelled at, it was compartmentalizing. He had no problem waking up in the morning, getting dressed and ready and heading into the office. He had no problem putting his head down and focusing on work all day, not letting a single thought of Juliet or the baby throw him off his stride.

It was only once he returned home to his big, quiet, empty brownstone that he lacked enough distractions to keep those thoughts from popping straight to the forefront of his brain and taking up residence like characters on a movie screen.

There was no fire in the hearth of his study, but that didn't keep him from taking a seat in front of it and cracking open a fresh bottle of scotch while he stared at the unlit logs and let the liquor's heat kick down his throat and into the pit of his stomach. At the rate he was going with this evening ritual of his, he figured he might have to buy stock in his favorite drink manufacturer or acquire a distillery and start making his own.

He remembered another night spent in this room not so very long ago. There had been a fire blazing bright in the fireplace then, snow falling lightly outside, but instead of scotch, they'd been drinking wine.

It had been one of the nights he and Juliet had agreed to meet after work in secret, even though she'd already called off her engagement. There was no reason to sneak around any longer, but she'd insisted.

She'd arrived by taxi, wearing a long coat, hat, a scarf and a pair of dark, large-rimmed sunglasses similar to the ones he'd bought for her to wear to the doctor's office even though they were hardly needed on a dreary winter evening. He'd met her on the stoop, sweeping her inside and into his arms for a deep, mouthwatering kiss. Kicking the door closed with his foot, he'd lifted her up Rhett Butler–style and carried her to his room, never taking his lips from hers.

They'd made love fast and furiously that first time. Hot and desperate and passionate. Hell, maybe it had been even twice…as much as they'd tangled up the sheets and steamed up the windows, and as many times as they'd rolled around, switching places, lingered and then started over, the exact details were a little blurry.

What was crystal clear in his mind, however, was the silken smoothness of Juliet's flesh beneath his hands and mouth. The musky floral scent of her perfume and hair and natural essence. The way she felt in his arms and how *he* felt when he was with her, inside her, lying next to her in the aftermath.

And he remembered how comfortable he'd been with

her even when they weren't making love. Talking on the phone late at night when no one else was around, or hearing her voice over his office line in the middle of the day. Sitting across from her at his kitchen table while they raided the refrigerator to fill their bellies after the rest of their bodies were thoroughly sated.

Which was how they'd ended up in his study, sharing a bottle of wine in front of the fireplace. As though it were yesterday, he remembered the ivory camisole and panty set she'd been wearing beneath one of his wrinkled dress shirts, and the black silk pajama bottoms he'd stepped into before they'd come downstairs.

After grabbing something to eat, he'd collected the wine and their glasses and carried them into the study, where he'd found a spot on the rug in front of the fire and sat with his back against the base of one of the leather armchairs. Juliet had waited while he poured more of the rich chardonnay, then lowered herself into the crook of his legs.

She'd snuggled back against his chest, her head resting on his shoulder, and it had been the most natural thing in the world to bring his arms up and wrap them around her waist.

He didn't know how long they stayed that way, simply enjoying the silence, the crackle of the hearth, the occasional sip of wine and each other. As far as he was concerned, everything had been just about perfect. He'd even been thinking that he wouldn't mind having Juliet around more, maybe on a permanent kind of basis.

That wasn't something he'd considered since Valerie had walked away with their child. He'd dated, had numerous short-term affairs, but never once had the idea of making any one of those relationships long-term crossed his mind.

Then came Juliet. The wrong woman at the wrong time. Rife with conflict and secrets and lies. Yet he couldn't seem to stay away from her.

So maybe he shouldn't try. She was the one woman he could actually see himself spending the rest of his life with, so maybe it was time to cut out the minutiae. Maybe it was time to look beyond his past, her present, all the things that kept them apart on paper. In reality, it was probably only a matter of reprioritizing and deciding that this—whatever it was between them—was worth fighting for.

He cleared his throat, shifted slightly, preparing himself for the whole we-need-to-talk, let's-take-the-next-big-step speech when Juliet twisted sideways in his lap so that her legs draped over his half-bare thigh. He moved with her, adjusting to the new position with a raised knee and one arm behind her back. She rested against them, easy and comfortable.

"Reid," she said softly.

"Mmm-hmm?"

He knew what he wanted to say to her—well, in general terms, if not the exact wording—but if she had something on her mind, he was happy to talk about that first. Maybe it would buy him some time and help him get his own thoughts in order.

She took a deep breath, one he felt shudder through her delicate frame, and he held her closer, rubbing her arms in case she was growing chilled.

Without looking at him, she said, "You can't know how much all of this has meant to me. Being here with you, spending time together."

He tightened his hold on her even more. She might be getting cold, sitting on the floor in little more than her underwear, despite the fire burning only a few feet away, but he was rapidly growing warm with contentment.

Sadly, the sensation didn't last long.

"But I can't see you anymore," she added, dousing him with the verbal equivalent of a cold shower in Antarctica.

"I'm sorry," she said, twisting to face him while he sat as still as a marble statue. "We knew this was only temporary and probably shouldn't have started in the first place. It's time to stop."

Shock and numbness gave way to understanding and the white-hot charge of anger. "You're going through with it, aren't you?"

"What?"

"The wedding. To that jackass."

Juliet pulled away, climbing carefully to her feet. "No, that's not what this is about."

"Really?" he asked sharply, disbelief evident in his tone. He pushed himself to his feet, standing mere inches from her. He wanted to reach out and grab her, but curled his hands into fists at his side instead, afraid he might shake her if he touched her at all. Either that or kiss her stupid so she would stop all this nonsense talk about leaving.

"Of course not. It's not a contest, Reid. If it were, you would have won. I called off the wedding and broke up with Paul to be with you these past several weeks."

"And now you're breaking up with me."

"What do you want from me, Reid? I told you from the beginning that we couldn't let this get serious. What would people think if they found out I've been spending all this time with you when I still haven't made it public that I broke the engagement with Paul? As far as my friends and family are concerned, they're just waiting for the invitations to arrive."

"So you're ashamed to let anyone know you're involved with me," he bit out with no small amount of bitterness.

"No!" With a huff, she put her hands on her hips. "For heaven's sake, it doesn't have anything to do with you. Not really. It's…the timing, and…everyone's expectations."

She paused and took a deep breath, her chest lifting beneath his unbuttoned shirt and the silky material of her camisole. When she spoke again, her voice was softer, almost apologetic.

"My entire life, I've always done what my parents asked me to, what they expected of me. Zoe has always been a wild child, Lily is a free spirit, but I was their 'good little girl.' Maybe because I'm the eldest, I don't know. But you have no idea how hard it was for me to work up the courage to quit my job in Connecticut and move here to work with Lily designing handbags. I was terrified of disappointing my mom and dad. And even though they accepted the decision, I don't think they were very happy about it, which just made me feel more guilty."

She sighed. "I haven't even told my parents yet that I called off the wedding. They're going to be furious, and can you imagine how much worse it will be if they find out I've been playing house with you while I'm *supposed* to be preparing to walk down the aisle with Paul?"

Shaking her head, she wiped her palms nervously down the outsides of her bare thighs. "I'm sorry, but I can't deal with it. If things were different... If we'd met and started our little tryst months after Paul and I were history, it wouldn't be so bad. But I can't deal with them doing the math and figuring out that we hooked up before my broken engagement was even cold...or worse yet, the truth—that the engagement wasn't quite as broken as it should have been when we started seeing each other."

Her hands stopped moving against her thighs and she crossed her arms, hugging herself. He watched the muscles of her throat roll as she swallowed. "Maybe later, after things settle down," she said barely above a whisper, "we could reassess and start seeing each other again. We could try for normal instead of sneaking around."

Reid scowled, remaining deathly still where he sat on the floor for fear of what he might do if he stood up. "Don't do me any favors."

The color leeched from her face. "Please don't be like that. You knew this is how things would end," she told him quietly, her light blue eyes apologetic but determined. "And I don't want to spend our last moments together fighting."

It was the *please* that did it. The *please* that got him to bite his tongue. To remain silent instead of raging about the bad decision she was getting ready to make or the kick to the gut she'd delivered just as he was prepared to bare his soul and ask her to stay with *him*. Good thing she'd stopped him before he'd put that foot in his mouth, wasn't it?

The silence that filled the room was so heavy it was

almost painful to bear. But he knew if he opened his mouth to say anything, it would be something he'd live to regret. So he kept his lips pressed tight, teeth clenched so hard he was afraid they might snap.

After a while, when she realized he wasn't going to say anything more, Juliet dropped her arms, shoulders following suit as she sighed. Without a word, she shrugged out of his shirt and draped it carefully over the back of the armchair, then lowered her chin and padded quietly out of the room.

For all he knew, she'd been pregnant even then. Looking back, he shouldn't have let her go. He should have gone after her, continued to fight, hashed it out with her once and for all until she saw reason and decided to stay with him.

But he hadn't. He'd stood there in the study, listening as she climbed the stairs to the bedroom, where she'd gotten dressed and collected the few items she had at his place, then come back downstairs and walked out.

Out of his house, out of his life…but never quite out of his mind. Or his heart.

What little light reached him from the lamp on his desk glinted off the amber liquid in the highball glass in his hand as he shook off the clinging bleakness of the memory. Reid turned it this way and that, playing with the different facets and angles.

Having Valerie walk out on him all those years ago had been painful. He'd felt as though the rug had been yanked out from under him because he'd let himself make plans. Plans to marry her, settle down, start a family. All in the natural order, things going along as he'd always expected them to.

But even then, the worst part had been the loss of his child. A child he'd never met, but who'd still left a tiny hole in his soul when he was taken away. He hadn't known for years that the child had been born and was out there somewhere, being raised by another man. But that only changed the sense of loss; it didn't necessarily make it better or worse.

Now, though, there was an ache in his chest that just wouldn't go away. It had started the night Juliet told them they were through and walked out of his life... he'd thought forever. The moment he'd realized she was no longer going to be in his life. Filling his house with her soft voice and feminine laughter. Giving him something—some*one*—to look forward to at the end of the day, somebody significant to talk with and confide in about more than business and the weather.

The ache was still there when he'd tracked her down at her family's lake house, though he'd done his best to hide it, ignore it, spackle over it so the pressure didn't weigh him down and keep him from functioning.

Then she'd told him she was pregnant, and the steady throb had changed to something warm and comforting. Almost like...hope. He was getting a second chance at all those things he'd given up on so many years ago.

He was also getting a second chance to be with Juliet, which he'd wanted all along.

But the ache was sharper now. Vast, throbbing, worse than ever. And somehow he couldn't see it going away or getting better over time. This time, he was pretty sure the trauma was permanent.

Because—as it had clearly taken him much too long to acknowledge, even to himself—she *mattered* to him. With or without a baby between them, it was Juliet who'd strolled in and changed the status quo. She'd changed *him*—inside and out.

A beat passed. Another flicker of light across the surface of his scotch. Another jolt of heat from his throat to his stomach as he threw back the liquor and contemplated pouring another.

He'd thought he could forget her, put the fevered passion of their affair behind him and go back to his normal, quiet life. The problem was, he didn't want to put it behind him this time or pretend it didn't bother him. He didn't want to let Juliet go or see his child only on weekends.

To hell with that, all the way around. A baby, it turned out, was just the justification he needed to turn this situation on its head.

Glass clinked as he set his drink none too gently on the table at his elbow and climbed to his feet.

Juliet had walked out on him twice now, and both times he'd let her go.

She wasn't going to get a third chance.

When Reid showed up at the door of Juliet's loft, he was as sober as a judge and wasn't about to put up with any bull. He'd had a meeting early that morning that hadn't gone very well, and now this.

He probably should have put it off another day or two. Or at least another few hours, until he was in a moderately better mood. But he was dressed to impress—charcoal slacks and suit jacket, light blue shirt and dark blue tie, all pressed and polished and professional—and figured putting his best foot forward with Juliet wasn't the worst idea in the world.

Raising his hand, he rapped his knuckles against the

dark gray of the reinforced-metal door. He waited and was about to knock again when it opened.

He'd expected Juliet or one of her sisters to answer, but instead, Reid found himself standing face-to-face with Lily's fiancé, Nigel Statham. Reid had had a number of interactions with the man because of his involvement in the investigation into the theft of Lily's designs. The theft had come from inside the California branch of the U.K.-based Ashdown Abbey, which the Statham family owned and Nigel was currently running.

Reid certainly hadn't anticipated seeing the man here, though. And from the looks of it, Reid was interrupting something.

Nigel's shirt was untucked and had clearly been re-buttoned with haste and a lack of precision, leaving the tails uneven. The fact that they were untucked at all was telling enough, given what he knew of the strait-laced Brit.

Reid cleared his throat, feeling suddenly awkward and intrusive. The chances of Juliet being at the loft while her sister and her sister's fiancé were in the middle of…what they were obviously in the middle of was unlikely. But since he was here and had already stepped in it, it would have been even more peculiar not to go ahead and ask.

"Hey," Reid said. "Sorry to, um… Yeah, sorry." He let the apology drop with a man-to-man shrug of the shoulder.

"I came to talk to Juliet," he continued. Then, already knowing the answer, he said, "I don't suppose she's here."

"No," Nigel responded. "It's just…"

He trailed off as Lily came to stand at his side. Her

hair was mussed, and her buttons were in no better shape than her fiancé's.

"Just the two of us," Nigel finished.

Reid nodded in understanding.

"I don't think Juliet wants to see you right now," Lily told him quietly.

To his surprise, she didn't sound defensive or angry. Even her expression was soft, almost sympathetic.

"She's been through a lot," Lily added. "She needs some time to herself."

"I know," he replied, digging deep for a modicum of calm. After all, Lily wasn't the Zaccaro he had big, fat issues with. "But I need to talk to her."

Lily lifted her gaze to her fiancé. They exchanged a glance, Nigel finally lifting a shoulder as if to say *it's your call.*

Reid frowned, his voice harsher than he intended when he said, "She's carrying my child. Don't you think that buys me a little consideration?"

Nigel's arm went around Lily's waist and he tugged her protectively close, making Reid feel like a first-class heel. Judging by the confusion on the other man's face, he didn't know any of the details behind Reid and Juliet's relationship, but without a doubt he was going to step in and back Lily no matter what.

Reid could respect him for that, but if he had to reach out and shake Juliet's sister to get the information he needed, then he would do it. Or at least get as far as he could before Nigel put him on his ass. Which was no less than he would do if their situations were reversed.

He tried once more for the calm and reasonable approach. Meeting Lily's blue eyes, which were just a couple shades lighter than Juliet's, he let her see his sincerity and quite frankly, his need.

"Please," he whispered.

A few seconds passed, and then she let out a sigh.

"She's not here, in New York," Lily said. "She and Zoe went to Connecticut to visit our parents. And I think Juliet wanted to patch things up with Paul."

Twelve

Reid gripped the steering wheel, his speed hovering well above the legal limit. The prospect of getting pulled over wasn't even a blip on his radar, however.

His blood pressure was too high, his mind cluttered with what Lily had told him back at the loft.

So Juliet wanted to patch things up with Paul, did she?

His teeth gnashed together so hard he expected them to turn to dust.

What had happened to her declaration that she was through with that misogynistic jackass? Or that said jackass wouldn't want anything to do with her now that she was pregnant with another man's child?

Then there had been Lily's parting shot and reminder that she didn't think Juliet wanted anything to do with him at the moment. That she needed some space, needed some distance, wanted to be alone. Translation: she wanted to stay far away from him.

Well, too damn bad. They'd had an understanding of sorts. In addition to saying she was done with the ex-fiancé, she'd claimed he would have total access to his child and full disclosure on the pregnancy.

Taking off without warning to parts unknown—aka Connecticut—was a breach of that accord, as far as he was concerned.

He hadn't bothered arguing with Lily or filling her in on his so-called agreement with her sister. It was none of her business, and she was never *not* going to be on her sister's side about every little thing, anyway.

He'd left Lily and her fiancé to whatever they'd been doing before he knocked on the door and headed back to his car, loosening and stripping off his tie in angry jerks along the way.

Crossing town to his office, he'd avoided stopping to converse with anyone, bypassing employees and cubicles until he could close himself in behind his desk and look up the address for Juliet's parents' home in Connecticut. It would have been easier to simply ask Lily for it, but then she would have called Juliet and told her he was on his way, and he didn't particularly want her to have advance warning of his arrival. He also could have called and asked his personal secretary for the information, but hadn't particularly wanted anyone in the office knowing what he was up to or asking questions about his absence later.

Jotting the address on a slip of paper, he exited his office again, telling Paula to clear his schedule "for a while" before taking the elevator downstairs and climbing back behind the wheel of his Mercedes. He entered

the Zaccaros' address into his GPS and took off, amazed
he didn't chew through his seat belt and half the dash-
board before he managed to make it out of the city.

Now there were only mere tenths of a mile left until
he reached the Zaccaro estate, and his internal temperature hadn't lowered a single digit. He was all but
steaming from the ears.

He also had no idea what he was going to say to Juliet when he saw her, he just knew he needed to get his
temper under control before that happened. He was *not*
her ex, and he was never going to be, no matter how
furious or frustrated he might get with her.

Pulling up the long, circular driveway, he came to
a stop several yards from the front of the sprawling
white house with its black shutters and pristine, brightly
blooming flower beds.

He cut the engine and sat there for a while, waiting
for some sense of Zen tranquility to wash over him.
Which, of course, didn't happen. The best he could
manage was a slow, even inhale and exhale and a small
amount of mental clarity.

Go to the door, lay things out for Juliet in straight-
forward, no-nonsense terms. Let her think it over, and
if his point of view didn't work for her, go to court and
fight for his right to see his child.

It wasn't his first choice by a long shot, but he wasn't
going to sit back and watch the same thing happen with
Juliet and the son or daughter she was carrying that
had happened with Valerie and the son he hadn't even
known had been born until years later. Not when what
he felt for Juliet was a thousand times stronger than
anything he'd ever experienced with Val.

He got out of the car and crossed the paved drive to

the redbrick front porch with its tall white pillars on either side of the door. His footsteps were the only sound other than a gentle breeze blowing through the nearby trees until he raised a hand and pressed the doorbell. He heard the muted chime from inside the house, and wondered at the intense pounding behind his rib cage as he waited for someone to answer.

Once again, he was prepared to find Juliet on the other side, and once again he was confronted by a different Zaccaro sister instead. This time, it was Zoe. She was smiling when she opened the door, but the minute she saw him, her blue eyes went ice-cold and her mouth turned down in a frown that was only one short trip away from a glare.

He blew out a breath and thought, *Here we go again.*

"Hello, Zoe," he said by way of greeting, making sure to keep his tone low and almost sickeningly polite. The last thing he needed was to give this sister more reason to be wary of or upset with him and go into full gatekeeper mode. He had enough negatives stacked against him already, thank you very much.

She didn't respond, merely crossed her arms over her chest and tapped the toe of one of her glittery stacked heels. She was a little underdressed for visiting her folks, he thought, taking in her tight dress and the amount of skin left bare both above and below the slinky material.

But of course she hadn't asked for his opinion, and he sure as hell wasn't going to give it. Not when he was trying to make nice and extract information from a woman who was quickly taking on some of the less attractive characteristics of an out-of-control pit bull.

"I'm looking for your sister, Juliet," he said, as

though any part of that explanation for his presence was actually necessary.

"I know who you're looking for," she snapped, the tapping of her foot growing faster and louder. "I just don't think she wants to see you."

Reid's jaw clenched, molars fusing together as he fought to hold on to his temper. He was getting *really* tired of hearing that.

He took a deep breath, nostrils flaring as he counted to ten. Through his teeth, because he just couldn't get them to part *that* much, he said, "Would you please tell her I'm here and let her make that decision on her own?"

Zoe's eyes narrowed. She looked him up and down, freezing him with her snooty-rich-girl stare.

Finally, she seemed to relax the slightest bit. Her arms loosened, her self-designed daZZle heels stopped clicking against the foyer floor and she tipped her head to one side.

"She's not here right now," Zoe said softly. "She went out for a while."

"Do you mind if I ask where she is?" he asked, matching her steady tone.

For the first time, indecision crossed the younger woman's face. Then she gave a growl of frustration.

"Fine. She went to see Paul. I tried to talk her out of it, at least temporarily, and even offered to go with her. But she insisted and said it was something she had to do alone."

Reid could feel his ire beginning to rise again. His fingers curled at his sides. He'd hoped to catch her before she "patched things up" with the bastard, though what he'd planned to do or say to keep that from happening, he didn't know.

He sucked a great gulp of air into his lungs, letting it out slowly at the same time he forced his hands to relax.

In a low voice that almost didn't sound like his own, he said, "Will you tell me where he lives so I can go talk to her? Hopefully before she makes a monumental mistake."

Zoe tipped her head in the other direction. After a second, she asked, "Will you promise not to hurt her?"

He leaned back as though he'd been punched, eyes going wide. "I would never lay a hand on her," he responded. Passionately. Sincerely. With more than a hint of affront.

"There are a lot of ways to hurt someone," Zoe said quietly. "Not all of them leave bruises."

If her question caught him off guard, that comment jolted him right down to the soles of his Italian-leather oxfords.

"You're right. And I promise," he said softly. "I'll do my level best not to hurt her."

It took another couple tense minutes for her to decide, but then she straightened, uncrossed her arms and rattled off the address of Juliet's ex-fiancé. The man Reid was going to try really hard not to put in traction.

As Juliet stepped out of the house, tugging the door closed behind her, the only thing she could think was that she had overdressed for the occasion. She'd wanted to look nice, but not too nice. Definitely not suggestive in any way, but not too casual or uncaring, either.

She'd opted for a cute little sundress from her sister's summer collection and a pair of burnt-orange espadrilles—not Zoe's creation, she had to admit—that matched the giant poppies on the dress's skirt. It was something she would have worn to the shop or out to lunch, or even just to work in the loft's design studio on a day when she was feeling bright and sunny.

But today, it had been a waste of time to try to look even halfway presentable. A total waste of makeup, as Zoe would say.

The click of the latch at her back carried a weight of finality, yet it didn't bother her. She didn't particularly care.

And that was good. Better than good. It was a relief. Her ticket to freedom, really.

With a smile slowly spreading across her face, she took the three wide steps in front of her with a bit of a bounce and walked down the brick walk to the tree-lined street of the cozy, upscale neighborhood that had nearly become her home.

Stepping off the curb, she rounded the hood of her car with every intention of climbing in and driving back to her parents'. Maybe stopping at their favorite bakery along the way to pick up a cake or pie or a dozen of the shop's giant specialty cookies because she suddenly felt like celebrating.

But at the last minute, she raised her head and stumbled to a halt. Across the street, with the nose of his Mercedes pointing in the opposite direction of her own car, Reid stood there, leaning against the driver's side of the glossy black vehicle.

"Reid," she breathed in surprise. Maybe the day hadn't been such a waste of makeup after all. "What are you doing here?"

He pushed away from the car, letting his crossed arms drop, and strode in her direction.

"I came to see for myself," he said.

His cool tone was the first sign she had that this probably wasn't going to be a warm and fuzzy meeting. Which was a shame, because she'd actually been in a good mood, verging on almost warm and fuzzy, only a few seconds ago for the first time in a long time.

Her shoulders slumped a bit and her voice was resigned when she asked, "See what for yourself?"

"This." He tipped his head toward the sprawling colonial behind her. "That you couldn't wait to get back to your fiancé, even after you promised you wouldn't. Even knowing you're pregnant with *my* child."

Juliet opened her mouth to respond. She was ready to snap at him, to tell him that—pregnant with his child or not—he had no right to track her every move, to confront her at every turn, to accuse her of crimes she hadn't committed.

Then she paused, a sudden sort of serene realization washing over her.

"You're never going to trust me, are you?" she asked quietly, making it more of a statement than a question, since she already knew the answer. "After everything that's passed between us—baby or no baby, *ex*-fiancé or no ex-fiancé—you're always going to suspect me of something. You're always going to be waiting to interrogate me because you think I've been up to something behind your back."

She shook her head, gaze flicking toward the ground as a wave of sadness spilled over her. She hadn't envisioned a happily-ever-after future with Reid any more than she could see herself crawling back to Paul and being happy with him for the next fifty years.

But she and Reid were going to share a child. They were going to be in close, regular contact, probably for the rest of their lives. It would have been nice if those interactions could have been friendly and polite.

It seemed that wasn't going to be the case, though, and that hurt more than she would have thought.

"For the record," she told him, "I never promised not to see or speak with Paul again. But I *can* promise you that we're not getting back together. Even if I were interested—which I so *completely* am not—" she gave a roll of her eyes "—I doubt Paul would be any more. At least judging by the fact that he had another woman naked in his bed when I arrived. And not for the first time. Apparently he's been seeing other women all along. He took great satisfaction in pointing out that he'd been willing to marry me for appearances' sake, but he'd certainly never intended to give up his extra-curricular activities."

Reid's eyes widened a millimeter, and Juliet was inordinately pleased that she'd been able to shock him with that piece of information.

"That's right," she continued. "It looks like we've both moved on. And it's for the best, believe me. But I needed to apologize for what I did to him that day at the church. My actions were unacceptable, and even though he didn't deserve me, he didn't deserve that, either."

For long, drawn-out moments, there was nothing but tense silence between them. She didn't hear crickets, but there were a few birds in the trees whose chirping she could make out clear as a bell.

And then Reid exhaled, the sound drowning out the birds as he lowered his head and drove his fingers through his short, dark hair. After a minute, he lifted his gaze to hers. "You know, I promised your sister

I wouldn't hurt you," he said carefully. "Looks like I broke that vow right off the bat."

Juliet's heart gave a little lurch, but he didn't give her time to respond.

"I feel awkward having this conversation in front of your ex's house," he began, scowling slightly and then shifting from one foot to the other. "Is there someplace else we could go where we'd have a bit more privacy?"

There weren't a whole lot of options, given that they were both a state away from their respective homes.

"We could go back to my parents' house," she told him.

He curled his lip and wrinkled his nose at her suggestion, as though he'd caught a whiff of something that smelled unpleasant.

"Yeah, but your sister is there," he reminded her, letting her know exactly what he found so distasteful about her suggested location. Well aware of Zoe's temper and what she could be like when she got a pebble in her shoe, Juliet almost chuckled.

"We can enter through the back and go straight up to my rooms. No one even needs to know we're there."

He didn't look completely convinced, but finally gave an unenthusiastic nod. Leaning around her, he opened her car door and held on to the frame as she slid in behind the steering wheel.

"I'll follow you back," he said while she fastened her seat belt and pressed the ignition button that started the engine with a purr.

"Drive carefully. And no taking any wrong turns—you know I'll just track you down again," he added before closing the door and crossing the street to the driver's side of his Mercedes.

Thirteen

His care and concern surprised her after the way he'd first approached her. But if there was anything she knew for certain about Reid, it was that he hid his true solicitous nature beneath a hard, surly shell.

With Reid sticking close to her rear bumper, she led them out of Paul's neighborhood and back to the even more upscale area that housed a number of multimillion-dollar estates, her family's being one of them. She drove up the long, curved drive but bypassed the house entirely, coming to a stop on the far side of the extended garage where her father kept his prized 1967 Corvette coupe and 1962 Shelby Cobra under lock and key. There was no chance of anyone discovering her or Reid's car parked in the rear.

Cutting the engine and stepping out of the BMW, she waited for Reid to do the same. As he approached, she turned and walked up the short path that led to the back of the house. They entered and climbed a set of rear stairs to the long, empty hallway that led to the suite of rooms that had been hers all while she was growing up.

Through the first doorway was a sitting room that at one time had been decorated in bright pinks and purples, with posters of her favorite heartthrobs on the walls. It still amused her that her parents had been all right with their three daughters doing pretty much whatever they liked with their rooms, as long as the rest of the house remained *Better Homes and Gardens* picture-perfect. And that included Zoe's less-than-charming décor from her goth and emo phases.

Lily's and Juliet's teen preoccupations had thankfully been a bit more mainstream and less difficult to cover over later with fresh paint and wallpaper. The room they were in now was painted a lovely, much more mature peach with elements of cream. The sitting area also contained a love seat that faced a television and entertainment center, and an armchair surrounded by bookshelves.

Through the second, inside door was her bedroom, which still contained a canopy bed and a walk-in closet that held clothing choices that ranged from her pre-teens to some of last year's best Zaccaro designs. She just hadn't gotten the chance to go through and weed things out for donation yet. And frankly, there were some items that held childhood memories she wasn't ready to dispose of at all.

But Reid didn't need to see that portion of the suite in order to say whatever it was he felt still needed to be said between them. Setting her handbag on the seat of the armchair, she turned back to face him just as he closed the door behind them with a click.

"Is this private enough?" she asked.

He took a minute to look around before his gaze returned to focus on her.

"This will do," he remarked. "It's a nice room. And you're pretty good at sneaking in without anyone noticing. Did you used to slip out a lot when you were a kid?"

Juliet's mouth curled in a quick half smile. "I wasn't nearly as bad as Zoe was. She was the incorrigible one, to be sure."

Almost as though their minds were running on a similar track, her smile disappeared and they both grew serious at the same time.

Reid cleared his throat.

"Here's the thing," he said, picking up the conversation where they'd left off in front of Paul's house. "I didn't trust you."

Oh, my. So that was what it felt like to be sucker punched.

She wondered why people were so caught up on the idea of honesty, and why she'd been so all-fired eager to ask for it from him. Sure, it sounded good in theory, but damn it, sometimes the bald, unadulterated truth just plain *hurt*.

Swallowing back the painful emotions that threatened to swamp her, she braced herself, waiting for whatever else he had to say—that she might or might not want to hear—or for him to say nothing more at all.

Maybe this was it. Maybe it was just "I don't trust you," end of story, have a nice day and he would turn around and walk away. Part of her hoped he would do exactly that. It would be so much less excruciating than to pick, pick, pick at the scab like they were doing now.

Another part of her, though, wanted him to say something, almost anything else, just so he would stay a few minutes more. As soon as they parted ways, she had a feeling their relationship was going to change drastically. To never see each other again or see each other only on the days of their custody agreement when they met to pick up or drop off their child.

New memories would be created to crowd out and cover over the ones from the past. Indifference or possibly even animosity would replace passion, attraction, affection.

She, for one, had been well on her way to love. She didn't think she could have admitted that before now, but there it was. The truth, finally, staring her in the eye. Funny that she hadn't been able to see it until it was too late.

Pulling her out of thoughts that were quickly heading in a "poor me" direction, Reid reached for her hands, taking them in his own. Her head lifted in startlement.

She'd thought they were working on their goodbyes, not something that would lead to touching. But the minute his skin touched hers, tingling started at her fingertips and moved forward until it spread throughout her entire body.

"I *didn't* trust you, Juliet," he said again, "but that's because…I couldn't. I didn't realize until recently that I don't trust much of anyone. Maybe that's why I got into the private-investigation business to begin with."

He let his arms drop, taking hers with them so that they formed a sagging bridge between them.

"I've never talked about this before, never told anybody else," he began in a low voice.

His gaze was on her, but he didn't meet her eyes, as though he were uncomfortable about the subject at hand and concentrating hard on the words that came out of his mouth. Juliet remained perfectly still and silent, surprised enough that he was opening up to her, and not wanting to do anything to cause him to stop.

"There was another woman, a very long time ago. She got pregnant, and I did the right thing—I asked her to marry me. But it wasn't out of guilt or duty, not really. I wanted to marry her. To be a family, a father."

He swallowed, the Adam's apple riding up and then down again at the center of his throat, and his toffee-brown eyes were glossy with old memories and past disappointments.

"I thought that was what was going to happen," he went on, "but instead, Valerie said she didn't want to be a wife or a mother. She left town and I never heard from her again. It wasn't until years later, when I started digging around, that I discovered she'd had the baby after all. And married another man. So apparently, she *wasn't* all that opposed to the idea of being a wife and mother, she just didn't want to be those things with me."

Juliet's eyes widened, her mouth going dry with shock.

Reid had another child?

Oh, she'd heard the rest, about the other woman he'd been involved with, but she didn't particularly care about his old girlfriends. They'd both had past relationships; she'd been engaged when they met, for heaven's sake. But as long as those relationships stayed in the past—for both of them—they didn't concern her.

But the fact that he already had a child with a woman who had walked out on him and never bothered to tell him he was a father… That was…monumental.

She thought back to the night he'd told her they should get married after the doctor had confirmed that she was, in fact, pregnant and realized suddenly what it must have cost him to make such an offer. No, he hadn't exactly asked or done the hearts-and-flowers, on-bended-knee proposal thing, but considering that he'd been down this road before, it must have been beyond difficult for him to discover that another woman he'd been intimate with had become pregnant with his baby and then volunteer to "do the right thing," not knowing if she would go through with it or pick up and run just as the last woman had.

If Juliet had known, had had even a clue, she would have handled the situation so much differently.

"You…" she began, but then had to stop, shake her head in disbelief, swallow and begin again. "You have a child already? How old? A boy or a girl? What's his or her name? Do you see him…or her?"

Once the questions started, they just sort of poured out in a jumble. It was too much to ask all at once, and surely more than he wanted to share at this moment, but she couldn't help the rampant curiosity coursing through her veins.

"I'm sorry," she said, shaking her head again. It was so much to absorb when she hadn't expected to even *see* him again in the very near future.

"No, it's all right," he responded gravely. "I should have told you before."

Taking a breath, he said, "A son. Ten years old. His name is Theo." He paused for a moment as pain tightened the corners of his mouth. "But I don't see him, no. Valerie doesn't even know I looked them up. She has no idea I know she had the child and married another man."

"Oh, but Reid…" Juliet stepped closer, squeezing his hands in her own. "You deserve to meet him, to spend time with him, to be a father to your son. And he most certainly deserves to know you. He may have a father figure in his life, but he doesn't have his *real* father, and every child has the right to that."

Reid's fingers flexed around hers, and for the longest time he said nothing. From the granite set of his jaw and brightness of his gaze, she suspected he was fighting back some rather ragged, overwhelming emotions.

And as much as she wanted to know everything, wanted to help him reunite with his firstborn—if that was what he needed, and if there was anything she could actually do to facilitate such a reunion—she didn't want to push him. Not here or now.

He'd already opened up to her so much when she hadn't expected it at all, and he would tell her more when he was ready.

So she simply waited, letting him work through his thoughts and feelings while they remained close and connected.

Eventually, his chest trembled as he took in a deep, shaky breath, blowing it out again slowly. Then his eyes locked with hers, so full, dark and sincere that her own lungs hitched slightly.

"I'm telling you all of this because…when Valerie left, she took the future I *thought* I was going to have with her. The whole wife, kids, white picket fence, minivan part of the American dream. And without even realizing it, that caused me to stop trusting people.…

Women especially. I didn't want to get hurt again, but more than that, I didn't want to make plans and get my heart set on something only to have it torn away from me."

Releasing one of her hands, he brought his knuckles up to brush the line of her cheek. "That's why I thought what we had was perfect. Intensely passionate, but casual, and with the knowledge that it was going to end. Maybe not as soon as it did, but eventually. No strings, no commitments, no expectations."

He gave a short, humorless laugh. "It didn't work out that way, though. From the very beginning, I was head over heels for you. I'm not sure I fully realized it at the time, and if you'd asked, I would have denied it to my dying breath. But it was there, so clear it nearly steals my breath to think of it."

Juliet's own breath was turning thick and heavy in her chest, her eyes growing damp.

Had he just admitted he cared for her? Maybe even… loved her? She was afraid to move, exhale, to so much as blink for fear he would stop talking or, God forbid, change his mind and start to backtrack.

So she remained perfectly still, waiting and hoping he would say more, her muscles rigid as her nerve endings popped like kernels of corn in a kettle of too-hot oil.

"Even before you told me about the baby, I wanted to be with you. It took every ounce of self-control I had to sit in my office the day of your wedding and *not* race to the church to stop it from happening. And the only reason I went into the office at all on a Saturday was because I knew if I stayed home, there'd be no chance of me staying put. If your sisters hadn't shown up when they did to tell me you'd run off, I honestly don't know how much longer I'd have lasted, anyway. I was about to chew through my desk, imagining you walking down the aisle into the arms of another man."

Despite her determination not to move, she couldn't hold back a watery chuckle.

Reid smiled in return. And then he grew serious again. "When I think about Valerie leaving, I'm sorry things didn't work out. I'm even more sorry that I haven't been in Theo's life. But when I think about losing you…"

He shook his head, the tendons in his throat working as he swallowed hard. Untangling his fingers from hers, he cupped her elbows instead, tugging her just a fraction closer until only the slightest whisper of air could pass between them.

"It makes me crazy. My chest gets so tight I can barely breathe, and my heart stops beating altogether."

Juliet inhaled sharply. The moisture that had been prickling behind her eyes for the past few minutes suddenly spilled over to roll down her cheeks.

"Baby or no baby," he continued in a voice rough with emotion, "I'm in love with you, Juliet Zaccaro. I want to marry you, be with you forever, work on that whole home-hearth-and-family American dream I never thought I'd have. That is, if *you'll* have *me*."

She was crying in earnest now, giant tears running in rivulets down her face and messing up the makeup she really shouldn't have worn today. But though she suspected she was on her way to looking like a Halloween reject, she couldn't have cared less.

She was staring into the eyes of the man she loved, and he'd just told her he loved her, too.

"Of course I'll have you," she told him.

Resting her palms flat on his chest, she felt the pounding of his heart beneath the layers of fabric and flesh and muscle, and knew it matched the staccato beat of her own.

"I love you, Reid. I never could have gotten involved with you when I did, the way I did, if I hadn't already been headed pretty strongly in that direction. It broke my heart to walk away from you—both times—but I did it because I didn't think you felt the same about me, and I didn't want to start down the path of yet another convenient but loveless relationship that was likely to end in disaster."

Going up on tiptoe, she wrapped her arms around his neck and sighed as his slipped around her waist to hug her tight, picking her right up off the ground.

"Even if I hadn't found out I was pregnant," she said quietly against his neck, "I couldn't have gone through with the wedding. I don't want to be married to a man I'm not totally and completely in love with, or one who doesn't feel that way about me. And the only man I'm totally and completely in love with is you."

Reid leaned back to meet her gaze, his soft chocolate eyes so warm and inviting that if she was standing on her own two feet, she was pretty sure her knees would have buckled and she'd have melted into a puddle on the floor.

"I'm glad you're pregnant," he told her in return. "It will give me an excuse to rush you down the aisle and make sure you're wearing *my* ring on your finger for the rest of your life."

"I like that idea," she said. "Very much."

"So do I," he whispered against her lips before taking her mouth in a long, sultry kiss.

When they came up for air, she was boneless and very possibly mindless, as well. They were pressed together from chest to knee, and since he was the only thing keeping her upright at the moment, she hoped they stayed that way forever. Especially when having him wrapped around her like cellophane was one of her favorite pastimes.

"How would you feel about giving me a tour of your bedroom before your family realizes we're here?" he murmured against her lips. "I'm especially interested in testing out the bed."

She chuckled. "I think that could be arranged. But you do realize you're going to have to sit through dinner with my parents afterward, don't you? And we're going to have quite a bit of explaining to do."

Quite a bit, she thought with a silent snort. Talk about a big, fat understatement.

"Whatever it takes to win them over and make you my wife," he said as she turned and led him by the hand into the bedroom.

Since he wasn't actually interested in the room itself, he didn't bother looking around. They went straight to the bed and stood at its edge, facing one another. She tipped her gaze up to his and he lifted a hand to her cheek, stroking back and forth with the pad of his thumb.

"Thank you for giving me a second chance," he whispered, so close she could smell the last remaining hint of his cologne.

She knew he wasn't just talking about now; he was talking about the past and the present and the future.

A second chance to make right everything that had gone wrong and move forward into the best life either of them could ever have, as long as they were together.

Running her fingers through the silky hair at his temples, she held him tight and touched her forehead to his. "Thank you for not letting me get away."

"Never," he promised, his hands flexing at her waist. "Finding people is what I do, sweetheart. And I will *always* find my way back to you."

Epilogue

Juliet stood in front of the cheval glass in her bedroom at her parents' estate. Unlike the last time she'd worn this dress and been about to walk down the aisle, she was smiling. A wide, beaming smile she couldn't seem to dim or get under control.

She never would have imagined that she could look at the fairy-princess bridal gown her sister had designed for her and be filled with anything but bad memories. Yet here she was, dressed head to toe in the very same crepe and tulle, feeling happier than any woman had a right to be.

As usual, Lily had worked a creative miracle. Rather than ditch her original wedding dress or start from scratch to design another, she had deconstructed the gown to such a degree that pretty much the only thing the two versions had in common was the color—snowy, pristine white—and the basic materials.

She had changed the cap sleeves to narrow straps. Trimmed the skirt so that it no longer belled out but fell straight to the floor, with all of the layers of glorious tulle creating a bustle and train at the back instead. And most important, she'd turned the fitted bodice into more of an Empire waistline to accommodate Juliet's growing pregnancy.

She wasn't showing *that* much yet, Juliet hoped, but she was nearly three months along, and the telltale bump of her belly did tend to give her away. The magic Lily had worked with the gown, though, meant no one at the ceremony would know unless she told them, and the pregnancy wouldn't be noticeable later on in photographs.

Behind her, the door opened. She watched in the mirror as her sisters entered the bedroom from the attached sitting room.

"Whew," Lily said in an exaggerated tone, closing the door behind them. "She's still here."

"We thought you might be considering running away again."

"Ha-ha," Juliet replied deadpan, turning from the mirror to face them. "I have no intention of going anywhere until this knot is legally and very officially tied."

Lily smiled, moving to the vanity to gather the sprigs of fresh flowers that would be woven into Juliet's hair. "Glad to hear it. I think having you disappear before another one of your weddings would send Mother completely over the edge. She's down there ordering random guests to keep an eye on all the exits just in case."

Zoe snorted in amusement, but Juliet felt only a pang of guilt at what she'd put her parents through the last time around. And now again, with more wedding plans and the worry that she wouldn't follow through this time, either.

She wondered if her groom-to-be might be suffering the same unease.

"What about Reid?" she asked. "Is he expecting me to make a run for it, too?"

"I don't think so," Lily answered.

"He's too busy wearing a path in the study rug and checking his watch every five seconds," Zoe supplied.

Juliet's smile slipped a notch, her brows winging downward with a hint of worry. "Is he all right? He's not having second thoughts, is he?"

That would certainly be an ironic turn of events— the runaway bride finally ready to walk down the aisle only to be left at the altar by a runaway groom.

"I should say not." This from Lily as she stood at Juliet's back, arranging the flowers in her upswept hair. "He keeps asking where you are and how much longer until we get this 'damn show on the road.'"

Juliet chuckled at her sister's low-throated impression of Reid's growing impatience. As strange as it might sound, she took the description of his sour mood as encouragement. Clearly, he was as eager as she was to formalize their commitment to each other.

Her hand fell to the small rise of her abdomen, rubbing gently. Things were going to be so much different from this point on, but in the very best ways possible.

Not only were they about to join their lives as husband and wife, but soon they would be welcoming their very own little boy or girl into the world. And rounding out their happily ever after even more, Reid's son was back in his life.

At her encouragement, he'd contacted the child's

mother. The woman hadn't been thrilled at first by his unexpected reappearance, but after a series of phone calls, emails and text messages, she'd agreed to let Reid visit Theo. Since then, they'd managed to work out an amicable visitation schedule without getting lawyers and the court involved, and Valerie had even agreed to let Theo attend the wedding. The ten-year-old was going to be their ring bearer, and was absolutely adorable in his tiny tuxedo.

Lily patted her shoulders and turned her to once again face the full-length mirror. "There you go. You look amazing."

"Even better than last time," Zoe added from where she was leaning against one of the tall bedposts. She was twisting one foot back and forth on the four-inch heel of her self-designed bridesmaid shoe and idly checking her French tips.

"Thank you," Juliet said, used to Zoe's preoccupied manner.

"Ready to go?" Lily asked, handing her an artfully arranged bouquet of red and white roses wrapped in lace and interspersed with sparkling crystals that matched the ones on Juliet's gown.

"Oh, yes."

The smile was back on her face as the three of them left her suite of rooms and walked slowly through the house to the base of the winding stairwell. Lily made her stop and wait for a few minutes while Zoe ran ahead to tell their father the ceremony could start. It was his job to give Reid the go-ahead to take his place with the minister before returning to walk Juliet down the aisle.

A second later, the music began, played by a ten-piece orchestra set up in the backyard. Her mother—

once she'd gotten over Juliet's first failed wedding attempt and learned she was going to be a grandmother—had gone all out, taking over 100 percent of the wedding preparations as though she was a born event planner. She'd decided on the music and the flowers and the food for the reception, as well as converting the entire rear of the estate into a bridal tableau fit for a queen.

As stunning as it was, however, and as beautiful as she knew it would look in the pictures, Juliet didn't particularly care about the backdrop of the ceremony. All she wanted was to become Mrs. Reid McCormack, regardless of the day or time, who was in attendance or how nice their surroundings might be.

To the lovely instrumental strains of "The Wedding March," Juliet walked down the white fabric aisle on her father's arm. Tears of happiness prickled her eyes as she saw Reid waiting for her at the end, standing so straight and tall in his tailored black tuxedo. The lines of his handsome face softened with love as he looked back at her.

Finally, she was there, accepting a peck on the cheek from her father as he handed her over—physically and symbolically—to her husband-to-be. Reid clasped her fingers, giving them a gentle squeeze as he smiled down at her.

"You made it," he said softly, speaking directly to her despite the fact that the minister stood only inches away, waiting to begin, and more than a hundred guests were looking on in anticipation of the exchange of vows. "I didn't even have to run after you this time."

She gave a small shake of her head. "No more running," she promised. "Not when I'm exactly where I want to be."

If possible, his smile widened even more. And then, before the minister could say a word, before he'd gotten even close to pronouncing, "You may now kiss the bride," Reid pulled her close and did just that.

* * * * *

If you loved this story, don't miss a single novel in
PROJECT: PASSION,
a series from
USA TODAY *bestselling author Heidi Betts:*

PROJECT: RUNAWAY HEIRESS

Available now, from Harlequin Desire!

COMING NEXT MONTH FROM

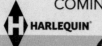
HARLEQUIN

Desire

Available February 4, 2014

#2281 HER TEXAN TO TAME
Lone Star Legacy • by Sara Orwig
The wide-open space of the Delaney's Texas ranch is the perfect place for chef Jessica to forget her past. But when the rugged ranch boss's flirtations become serious, the heat is undeniable!

#2282 WHAT A RANCHER WANTS
Texas Cattleman's Club: The Missing Mogul
by Sarah M. Anderson
Chance McDaniel knows what he wants when he sees it, and he wants Gabriella. But while this Texas rancher is skilled at seduction, he never expects the virginal Gabriella to capture his heart.

#2283 SNOWBOUND WITH A BILLIONAIRE
Billionaires and Babies • by Jules Bennett
Movie mogul Max Ford returns home, only to get snowed-in with his ex— and her baby! This time, Max will fight for the woman he lost—even as the truth tears them apart.

#2284 BACK IN HER HUSBAND'S BED
by Andrea Laurence
Nathan and his estranged wife, poker champion Annie, agree to play the happy couple to uncover cheating at his casino. But their bluff lands her back in her husband's bed—for good this time?

#2285 JUST ONE MORE NIGHT
The Pearl House • by Fiona Brand
Riveted by Elena's transformation from charming duckling into seriously sexy swan, Aussie Nick Messena wants one night with her. But soon Nick realizes one night will never be enough....

#2286 BOUND BY A CHILD
Baby Business • by Katherine Garbera
When their best friends leave them guardians of a baby girl, business rivals Allan and Jessi call a truce. But an unexpected attraction changes the terms of this merger.

YOU CAN FIND MORE INFORMATION ON UPCOMING HARLEQUIN® TITLES, FREE EXCERPTS AND MORE AT WWW.HARLEQUIN.COM.

HDCNM0114

REQUEST YOUR FREE BOOKS!
2 FREE NOVELS PLUS 2 FREE GIFTS!

HARLEQUIN®

Desire

ALWAYS POWERFUL, PASSIONATE AND PROVOCATIVE

YES! Please send me 2 FREE Harlequin Desire® novels and my 2 FREE gifts (gifts are worth about $10). After receiving them, if I don't wish to receive any more books, I can return the shipping statement marked "cancel." If I don't cancel, I will receive 6 brand-new novels every month and be billed just $4.55 per book in the U.S. or $4.99 per book in Canada. That's a savings of at least 13% off the cover price! It's quite a bargain! Shipping and handling is just 50¢ per book in the U.S. and 75¢ per book in Canada.* I understand that accepting the 2 free books and gifts places me under no obligation to buy anything. I can always return a shipment and cancel at any time. Even if I never buy another book, the two free books and gifts are mine to keep forever.

225/326 HDN F4ZC

Name _____ (PLEASE PRINT) _____

Address _____ Apt. # _____

City _____ State/Prov. _____ Zip/Postal Code _____

Signature (if under 18, a parent or guardian must sign) _____

Mail to the **Harlequin® Reader Service:**

IN U.S.A.: P.O. Box 1867, Buffalo, NY 14240-1867
IN CANADA: P.O. Box 609, Fort Erie, Ontario L2A 5X3

Want to try two free books from another line?
Call 1-800-873-8635 or visit www.ReaderService.com.

* Terms and prices subject to change without notice. Prices do not include applicable taxes. Sales tax applicable in N.Y. Canadian residents will be charged applicable taxes. Offer not valid in Quebec. This offer is limited to one order per household. Not valid for current subscribers to Harlequin Desire books. All orders subject to credit approval. Credit or debit balances in a customer's account(s) may be offset by any other outstanding balance owed by or to the customer. Please allow 4 to 6 weeks for delivery. Offer available while quantities last.

Your Privacy—The Harlequin® Reader Service is committed to protecting your privacy. Our Privacy Policy is available online at www.ReaderService.com or upon request from the Harlequin Reader Service.

We make a portion of our mailing list available to reputable third parties that offer products we believe may interest you. If you prefer that we not exchange your name with third parties, or if you wish to clarify or modify your communication preferences, please visit us at www.ReaderService.com/consumerschoice or write to us at Harlequin Reader Service Preference Service, P.O. Box 9062, Buffalo, NY 14269. Include your complete name and address.

HD13R

Nate's brow furrowed, his eyes focused on her tightly clenched fist. "Put on the ring," he demanded softly.

Her heart skipped a beat in her chest. She'd sooner slip a noose over her head. That was how it felt, at least. Even back then. When she'd woken up the morning after the wedding with the platinum manacle clamped onto her, she'd popped a Xanax to stop the impending panic attack. She convinced herself that it would be okay, it was just the nerves of a new bride, but it didn't take long to realize she'd made a mistake.

Annie scrambled to find a reason not to put the ring on. She couldn't afford to start hyperventilating and give Nate the upper hand in any of this. Why did putting on a ring symbolic of nothing but a legally binding slip of paper bother her so much?

Nate frowned. He moved across the room with the stealthy grace of a panther, stopping just in front of her. Without speaking, he reached out and gripped her fist. One by one, he pried her fingers back and took the band from her.

She was no match for his firm grasp, especially when the surprising tingle of awareness traveled up her arm at his touch.

He held her left hand immobile, her heart pounding rapidly in her chest as the ring moved closer and closer.

"May I, Mrs. Reed?"

Her heart stopped altogether at the mention of her married name. Annie's breath caught in her throat as he pushed the band over her knuckle and nestled it snugly in place as he had at their wedding. His hot touch was in vast contrast to the icy cold metal against her skin. Although it fit perfectly, the ring seemed too tight. So did her shoes. On second thought, everything felt too tight. The room was too small. The air was too thin.

Annie's brain started swirling in the fog overtaking her mind. She started to tell Nate she needed to sit down, but it was too late.

Don't miss
BACK IN HER HUSBAND'S BED
by Andrea Laurence,
available February 2014 from
Harlequin® Desire wherever books are sold!

HARLEQUIN®

Desire

ALWAYS POWERFUL, PASSIONATE AND PROVOCATIVE.

Nothing's come easy to Chance McDaniel ever since his best friend
betrayed him. And when the deception explodes into a
Texas-size scandal, his best friend's sister, Gabriella del Toro, shows
up in town to pick up the pieces and capture his heart..

But will the web of deception her family has weaved ensnare
her yet again?

Look for **WHAT A RANCHER WANTS**
from Sarah M. Anderson next month
from Harlequin Desire!

Don't miss other scandalous titles from the
Texas Cattleman's Club miniseries, available now!

SOMETHING ABOUT THE BOSS
by Yvonne Lindsay

THE LONE STAR CINDERELLA
by Maureen Child

TO TAME A COWBOY
by Jules Bennett

IT HAPPENED ONE NIGHT
by Kathie DeNosky

BENEATH THE STETSON
by Janice Maynard

Available wherever books and ebooks are sold.

Powerful heroes…scandalous secrets…burning desires.

HD73295